HAUNTED
BOSTON

Behind every man now alive stand thirty ghosts, for that is the ratio by which the dead outnumber the living.

Arthur C. Clarke, Space Odyssey

HAUNTED
BOSTON

Gemma King

The
History
Press

An aerial view over Boston town featuring South Street – one of the town's paranormal hotspots - with seven haunted locations either on the street itself, or a stone's throw from it. (Courtesy of Dan Watts)

First published 2013

The History Press
The Mill, Brimscombe Port
Stroud, Gloucestershire, GL5 2QG
www.thehistorypress.co.uk

Typesetting and origination by The History Press
Printed in Great Britain

CONTENTS

ABOUT THE AUTHOR

GEMMA King has lived in Spalding for many years, and since the release of her first book *Haunted Spalding*, her interest in historic sites and the paranormal has led her to become a keen visitor of Boston.

Whilst Gemma's interest in paranormal phenomena dates back to her childhood, at the age of nineteen her curiosity about the subject was further fuelled when she had a ghostly experience of her own, and by this time she had already done much research into the field of the paranormal and different types of ghost manifestation. Now in her thirties, she has carried out many investigations in Spalding, Boston, Peterborough, and further afield. She is known locally for her interest in the paranormal and has been invited to give talks about her experiences. Having no psychic ability, her investigative work is conducted scientifically and objectively with the use of specialist equipment and techniques, and her ultimate aim has always been to capture irrefutable

evidence of ghosts that would convince a sceptic of their existence. Throughout the course of her work she has also been able to offer assistance to people seeking insight or advice in relation to paranormal activity and has always found that aspect of her investigation work by far the most rewarding.

ACKNOWLEDGEMENTS

IN compiling this book, many people assisted me in different ways and I would like to take this opportunity to thank them.

Firstly, I would like to give special thanks to my husband Phil and my two children Mikey (six) and Jasmine (five) for their unwavering patience and support during my busy periods of research, investigating and writing. In addition to his support of my project, Phil has also provided crucial assistance with some of my illustrations. I am very grateful for his invaluable contribution.

Special thanks also go to my parents Lin and Den, my sister Melissa and brother-in-law Daniel and the rest of my family and close friends, who have always supported me in my passion for all things paranormal and who have offered so much encouragement over the years with my research, investigations and more recently with my compilation of this book. Furthermore, my brother Daniel Watts worked extremely hard on my behalf in filming and putting together promotional videos in relation to this

book, and big thanks also go to him. Also to Chloe Watts, an aspiring young investigator whose assistance has proved invaluable during site tours and investigation nights, and Serena Watts, who has also assisted and supported me in not only my investigations but also my many talks.

Huge thanks to Dean Grant and his investigation team 13 Paranormal for their assistance in exploring some of the most haunted sites in Boston. They are a highly skilled investigation team and have been amazing to work with. It is always a wonderful learning experience working with different investigators, as everyone works differently and even slight differences can prove really beneficial in learning new techniques and gaining experience in the field.

With regard to contributions and assistance with specific features in the book, thanks go to Andrew Malkin, Communications Manager at Boston Borough Council for the invaluable contribution to my research into the Guildhall, plus the exclusive photographs. Andrew and Chris Malkinson at The

Gliderdrome for their support in my research of the building and co-operation in allowing access to redundant parts of the building, no longer visited by the public – plus privileged access to their historic and exclusive photo collection. Mike Raymond, Theatre Director at Blackfriars for his valued time and support in assistance with my research, plus access to the building to conduct a paranormal investigation. Claire Sheldrake from Fydell House, who was extremely hospitable and helpful during my time researching the building and who also allowed the team to carry out a paranormal investigation. David Horry, Principal Leisure Services Officer at Geoff Moulder Leisure Complex for his insight and co-operation in my compilation of the book feature plus access granted to 13 Paranormal for their paranormal investigation. Thanks also go to Basil Wright (former employee of Norprint), who kindly granted me exclusive access to the former factory building and gave his time by leading me on a detailed and insightful tour.

I would like to give mention to Nigel Crowe and Shirley Elrick for their dedicated time and assistance in researching the history of the Jolly Crispin pub/bed and breakfast as the information they provided was extremely helpful.

Special thanks also go to Sandra and Jenny Sales, former owners of Church Key Studio, for their warmth, hospitality and assistance with my research. And to Carl from Silt Side Service Ltd for his giving me his valuable time and expertise.

I remain very grateful to Billy Jenthorn for access to his wonderfuly informative blog, which provided exclusive photographs of Boston in times gone by, and stories such as 'The Shaw Road Ghost', 'Tattershall Road' and 'Phantom Train on the A16'. Thank you to Gemma Gadd and the *Boston Standard*, who have allowed access to their archives and publication of their material, and also provided unwavering support for my *Haunted Boston* project from the outset.

Thank you also to Andrew Kilbee of Lincs-Paranormal and Editor of the *Boston Old Times* and Helen Shill for the insight and historic photographs that they have provided in connection with The Scala Theatre.

All photographs in this publication, unless otherwise stated, are copyright of the author. I have made every effort to contact copyright holders and gain permission for the use of any copyright material, but I apologise if I have inadvertently missed anyone out.

INTRODUCTION

LOCATED in the heart of the Lincolnshire fens, Boston is a town rich in medieval history. Having been one of the main ports for the international shipping trade, it was a busy market town as early as the twelfth century. In the thirteenth century, four orders of friars settled in Boston and some remnants of their establishments are still present today. While researching this book, I have explored locations in and around Boston where human remnants of the past still exist in the form of ghostly apparitions, spirit voices and other unexplained paranormal phenomena. I have investigated some of the most haunted locations in Boston in an attempt to communicate with the entities present, capture evidence of paranormal activity, and listen to their voices in order to try and establish why they are still around us, sharing our space and communicating with us. In researching the stories of ghosts in and around Boston I have uncovered a wealth of different testimonies, new and old. I have also drawn on both local history and contemporary sources to separate fact from folklore, in order to bring you chilling stories of ghostly activity that have never previously been told and exclusive photographs that have never previously been published. In addition to the book itself there is a website that runs concurrently (see Bibliography) where readers will be able to listen to EVP clips (spirit voices) and other events captured on audio in some of the locations, see some of my favourite photographs in more detail and look at some of the unpublished photographs. In view of the fact that my ultimate objective in investigating has always been to find out what is really going on and try to capture evidence of paranormal activity, I feel that the website feature is a unique and special way to do this, adding another dimension to the book which enables people to hear and see the evidence, as well as just reading about it.

Gemma King, 2013

1

INVESTIGATIONS

AS a paranormal investigator, I have explored many haunted locations over the years. As part of my research for this book, and in fulfilment of my hobby, some of the locations featured have been the subject of investigations and I have therefore opted to include this chapter, which gives insight as to how I conduct the process of investigating and the equipment and techniques that I personally recommend in order to achieve the best possible results.

Investigating on location. (Author's own photo)

The Basics

I always visit the location that I am planning to investigate before the planned investigation night, as this enables me to tour the building, familiarise myself with the surroundings, listen to the testimonies of activity that has taken place and give consideration to other possible causes of the activity that has been reported. For example, I take note of where fuse boxes and other power sources are located as this will affect electromagnetic field (EMF) meter readings. I also look for doors and windows where periodic draughts could be causing reported 'cold spots', or perhaps where sources of light penetrating through windows or building fabric could cause visual anomalies. Another thing I check for is general noise levels, although buildings and their surroundings are typically quieter at night. Investigations are usually conducted in the dark, so as to increase awareness of all the senses, and also because visual anomalies are best captured on night vision or with a camera flash. It is therefore vital that investigators are familiar with their surroundings. On the night of the investigation it is important that the building is locked down and noise contamination is kept to a minimum. After all, it is only when these factors are taken into account that we can consider the real possibility of paranormal activity occurring, and I want to stand the best possible chance of capturing the evidence.

Testimonies

I am always very interested in the particular testimonies that people give relating to their paranormal experience, and one of the things I am always keen to try and establish is whether the encounter they have had relates to a residual ghost or an intelligent spirit. Certain characteristics of a haunting can be quite telling at the testimony stage of the investigation process, in the sense that some people describe a visual spectacle that carries all the hallmarks of a residual ghost. If, for example, an apparition of a person in period costume was seen walking through a wall where a door was once located, seemingly completely unaware of their surroundings, this would suggest to me the likelihood of a residual ghost. These are most often seen walking through walls; across gardens; sometimes even above or below ground level – ground level may have changed since their lifetime – and they have no 'intelligence' or 'awareness' whatsoever because they are merely a replay of a past event; a visual spectacle. It is widely believed that traumatic events are most likely to lend themselves to residual playback, and there have been many experiences reported all over the world where people have witnessed the 'playback' of suicides or even murders known to have taken place many years before. Sometimes the experience is visual; sometimes it is audible and visual. Scientists have accepted the phenomenon of residual energy becoming captured in certain masonry materials such as slate, rusted nails and stone (rusted or oxidised materials) as they contain properties similar to those of videotapes, which have to go through an oxidisation process to enable the capture of visual/audible information. As yet, however, it is not known what triggers the release of the residual energy.

Another point that I always note in my initial consultation at a haunted location is the exact location(s) within the building where the paranormal events have occurred. This gives an idea of where would be the best place to set up digital video recorders (DVRs) and electronic voice phenomenon recorders to maximise the possibility of capturing evidence.

Equipment and Techniques

Base Reading Meter

This tests various measurements, and is used at the beginning of an investigation to test general levels of sound, temperature, electromagnetic field and sound levels in different parts of the building in order to get a 'base' reading, so that anomalies and variations of the base reading can be easily detected during the analysis of the data at the end of the night.

Investigation equipment. (Author's collection)

EMF Meter

Sometimes referred to as the KII, these detect levels of electromagnetic energy, which spirits use in order to manifest. The theory is that spirits take energy from sources of power such as appliances and lights in order to manifest in a remote space away from those power sources. For example, I was in a building, talking to the owners about how we can use EMF detectors to try and communicate with spirits by encouraging them to come towards you and touch the machine. On this particular evening, as I gave my demonstration, there was a notable dimming of surrounding wall lights, right on cue. Moments later the EMF meter flickered all the way up to red – as though the spirits were taking the energy from the wall lights and using it to light up my machine in the centre of the room. On many occasions, I have found that the machine lights up on request, and then goes back down to green when I ask the spirits to step away from it. Repeating this process is a good indication of possible interaction with an 'intelligent' spirit, and these can also be used to invite 'yes or no' answers from the entity that is communicating, so long as you explain to them what the machine is for, and what you would like them to do in order to interact with you.

It is also very important to offer reassurance to the spirit that you mean them no harm.

As well as confirming paranormal activity, EMF meters can also debunk it, in that some reputedly 'haunted' buildings have had various testimonies of activity, all reported to be emanating from the same room – it may be that the occupants of the room have all experienced feelings of paranoia as though someone is watching them – or they may have been experiencing feelings of nausea or seeing dark shadows.

These symptoms, whilst similar to those of a paranormal experience, can sometimes be attributable to high levels of EMF given off by nearby fuse boxes, exposed cables or appliances, and in such cases anyone spending lengthy periods of time in that room would more than likely be suffering the unpleasant effects of excessive exposure to EMF.

Motion Detectors

These can be positioned in a closed-off room while investigations are taking place elsewhere in the building. If they go off, it can be an indicator of a ghostly presence in that room. It is always good to note the time if that does happen, so you can review the event alongside other data such as audio and DVR footage. In fact, if you put talc on the floor, you can then check for footprints that don't match any of the investigation team.

EVP and Digital Voice Recorders

This is my personal favourite piece of equipment; its use has enabled me to capture what I would consider to be some of my most compelling pieces of evidence of possible interaction/communication from intelligent spirits. The theory is that recording devices can capture disembodied sounds and spirit voices known as 'Electronic Voice Phenomena', which are inaudible to the human ear at the time of recording but can be heard after the investigation, during playback of the recorded session. When playing back the session, specialised computer software is used to extract and analyse any anomalies in the recording. The average human voice is recorded within a frequency range of 500-3000Hz but spirit voices and other anomalies are captured on audio devices measuring at frequencies far beyond this

range. You can maximise the chance of capturing a good EVP during an investigation by introducing yourself and your equipment to any spirit entities present and inviting them to communicate with you. You then need to ask lots of questions, making sure an appropriate period of silence is left to allow for answers. It is also good to leave the voice recorder running during silent vigils to enable the capture of any random disembodied sounds. It is important to remember when using EVP recorders that they are very sensitive, and as such should be placed on a flat surface where possible and left untouched while investigating – it is also incredible how loud footsteps are when listening to the audio following an investigation, and for that reason it is also best to minimise walking about whilst recording. When it comes to playing back the audio after the investigation it is best to use good headphones and computer software that enables you to view the sound waves, identify anomalies and extract the clips where you have heard a voice or noise that cannot be considered to have come from any other person or source on the night. EVP clips can then be graded into three categories as follows:

Class A: Easily heard and understood from the speakers of a sound system.
Class B: Can be heard over the speaker but there may not be agreement as to the message – some words may be agreed on.
Class C: Can only be heard with headphones; these are often difficult to decipher.

To date I have had much success using the EVP recorder, and I feel they are a good validation of intelligent communication. For example, sometimes my statements or questions have been responded to

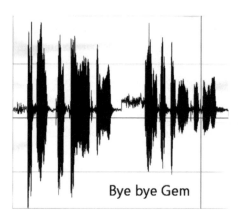

Bye bye Gem

This EVP of a young child's voice was captured at the end of an investigation night just as I was packing away equipment. I said 'Goodbye' to any resident spirits and this response, which I did not hear at the time, was audible upon playing back the recording. In this clip, the volume of the child's voice has been slightly increased to make it more audible, which is why the sound waves are raised from the centre. (Author's own photo)

by use of my name, which rules out the argument put forward previously by some sceptics that the sounds are merely interference from outside sources such as radio. The EVP recorder is extremely fulfilling in terms of my main objectives in paranormal investigation – to capture irrefutable evidence of spirit communication, and to present evidence that enables ordinary people such as myself, with no psychic ability whatsoever, to witness paranormal events and spirit communication for themselves rather than relying on what they are told by mediums.

Camera

I take a good quality camera on investigations, and I invite spirits to appear in my photographs. Doing so has produced some very good results, from large orb-like anomalies the size of a football to a half-bodied apparition. Pictures are best taken in a dark or a dimly-lit room as that will show up the anomalies better than in daylight. With regard to orbs, not

all balls of light will be ghostly manifestations – I have to rule out dust or other debris. However, it is believed that spirits need a lot of energy to manifest in full-bodied visual form and as such will often manifest as a ball of light. Spirit orbs are unmistakable in appearance with a ring formation around the edge. Some are also very large and very bright. I find the theory of orbs interesting, given that many people who have had near-death experiences have reported becoming an orb of light and quite often on investigations, pictures will show large ones that are clearly not insects or dust, due to their size and formation.

DVR

Digital Video Recorders can capture good evidence of paranormal activity, and they work well; either set up in one corner, perhaps a 'hotspot' where activity has previously been reported, or they can be taken around the building as you investigate. Either way, they can pick up both audio and visual anomalies – they ideally need to have a night vision setting, as investigation vigils are mostly conducted in the dark.

Trigger Objects

These are items that I take on investigations that are appropriate to the description of the ghost; they assist in engaging in communication. If a ghostly man has been seen in the building smoking a cigar I take a cigar with me – or if a child has been seen, I take small toys, relevant to the suspected time period of the ghost if possible. I set the items up at the beginning of the investigation night by placing them on a piece of paper, drawing around them, and periodically checking to see if they have moved.

Torches

A good torch is essential on an investigation, as all the lights are generally switched off. If the torch has a light button on the back of it, you can put it down on the floor and invite the spirits to switch it on and off.

Thermometers

Air and laser thermometers are good for noting a sharp drop in temperature, often caused when spirits manifest. Air thermometers are my personal favourite as they show the temperature of the space in front of you rather than the temperature of the ground or nearby surface. On some investigations I have known the temperature to drop several degrees upon request in one specific spot where an investigator felt cold or where the EMF detector had lit up.

Séances

I do not have any psychic or medium ability, and I investigate by using technology and specialist techniques on my quest to try and capture hard evidence of paranormal activity. In addition to this, I also conduct séances using a board and a glass to communicate directly with spirits.

Being scientific and objective in my approach to investigations, what I like the most about séances is that they do not seem to have any scientific explanation – one theory behind them has been that it's telekinetic energy (the power of the mind) that moves the glass to spell words – however, I refute that theory, given that telekinesis is a very rare ability and it would therefore be extremely rare for six people around a séance table

Team members taking part in a séance as part of the Blackfriars investigation. Left to right: Megan (Deputy Manager, Blackfriars), Steph (13 Paranormal), Dean (13 Paranormal), Pete (13 Paranormal), Chloe (Trainee Investigator). (Author's own photo)

to all have that skill. It has also been said that it is the power of the mind moving the glass towards a common goal – but in cases where no one around the table knows anyone else I cannot see how this could be the case, given the very specific information that comes through directed at just one person. It would not be possible to orchestrate the way the glass moves; when it glides across the board toward one particular person they are usually quite surprised. Often, the spirit that comes through would not be known by anyone else at the table, and the information that they give can be validated by the person with whom they have connected, with further open questioning about events and memories from their past together. What I also love is the fact that the séances can be pretty accurate; they can work as a two-way conversation, and everybody can see and feel the experience. The direct communication with spirit entities means that séances can often be a useful tool in providing answers for people in relation to paranormal activity in their home or place of work, as well as resolving situations where unhappy spirits are making their presence felt in a manner that makes the occupants of a building feel uncomfortable. One such case springs to mind where a resident child spirit came through to talk to the owner of a place we were investigating. It transpired that she had been trying to get their attention because she did not like the loud chimes on the clocks – she found them scary. The owner had many clocks and they covered the walls in one particular room; he agreed to turn off some of the chimes, which provided a resolution and a positive outcome for everyone concerned.

On some occasions during a séance we encounter a spirit that asks for our help because they are grounded, unable to move on, and this can happen for a number of different reasons. Through careful questioning we are able to work out the reason and assist them in moving on. I do not know how this works, but it does work and the feeling when this happens is immensely comforting and emotional for everyone. It is good to know that through séances we are seemingly able to assist trapped energies, often reuniting them with their family members who have by this time passed into spirit and will be waiting for them. Scientific as I am, I do believe in séances and the possibility that we can help people, here and in spirit, which reinforces my passion and belief in this investigative tool.

Whilst the use of the Ouija board is perceived by some people as controversial, I feel this perception is often based on movies and television dramas of times gone by, where their use invariably lends itself to some kind of horrific drama. It could also partly be due to the experiences of some people using them in previous decades when they were sold in shops as a recreational toy – I have no doubt that many people who have used the Ouija board over the years have not fully understood or respected the seriousness of this method of communication with spirits and as such may not have conducted themselves appropriately. The séances that I have conducted over the years along with members of my former paranormal investigation team are protected by an opening and closing-down prayer. Also, no one under the influence of alcohol is ever allowed to participate and anyone who-does take part must remain respectful of spirit energies that come through at all times – after all, spirit energies are people without bodies and should be respected as such.

I have worked with investigators who have been conducting séances for many years and I have never had a negative experience. That said, it is crucial that people know how to respond appropriately to any unpredictable communications from a spirit during a séance, and for this reason I would strongly advise that it is not something to partake in lightly. I would certainly not recommend anyone doing it unless they are with an experienced individual who knows how to conduct the séance properly and with the necessary protection.

13 Paranormal

I teamed up with paranormal investigator Dean Grant and his Boston based team, 13 Paranormal, in connection with some of the investigations for this book as they have much credibility and experience in the local area and also much further afield. Further details of Dean's team can be found at their website: www.13Paranormal.co.uk.

The 13 Paranormal team.

2

BLACKFRIARS THEATRE AND ARTS CENTRE

Located near to a medieval burial ground and taking its name from one of the four orders of friars that occupied the building in the late thirteenth century, Blackfriars Arts Centre is one of the few medieval buildings that still exists in Boston town.

Little has been recorded about the friary prior to 1288; however it is known that between the years of 1288 and 1309,

Blackfriars. (Author's own photo)

it was rebuilt having been largely destroyed by fire, started deliberately by rioters, which had spread across much of the town. Stones from Barnack and oak from Sherwood Forest were among the materials used in the construction of the new monastery and, when complete, there were 29 monks in residence, named Blackfriars because of the colour of their clothing. It is thought that the building as we know it now used to be the dining area for the monks.

Following the dissolution of the monasteries under the reign of Henry VIII it is thought that the building remained under royal ownership for some time, and in the centuries that followed, was gradually left to fall to ruin. As was the case with all unused buildings in Boston (a town with little in the way of trees), oak and stone from the former friary were taken elsewhere and used to construct shops. As a result of this practice, much of the original friary was dismantled and part of it became derelict. In 1935, however, the Boston Preservation Trust was formed and safeguarded the future of Blackfriars as an important part of the town's heritage.

In 1959, the decision was made to convert the building into a theatre for local arts and drama groups and, having secured funding and been transformed by an internal restructure, it finally opened its doors to the public for the first time in 1966. Since then, the hard work of volunteers has helped Blackfriars to evolve into the successful arts establishment that it is today and has secured it a place in the hearts of the local community.

Author's interpretation of the approximate area that would have been occupied by the friary buildings and burial ground in medieval times. (Imagery © 2012 DigitalGlobe, GeoEye, Get Mapping Plc, Infoterra Ltd & BlueSky, Map Data © 2012, Google, Phil King)

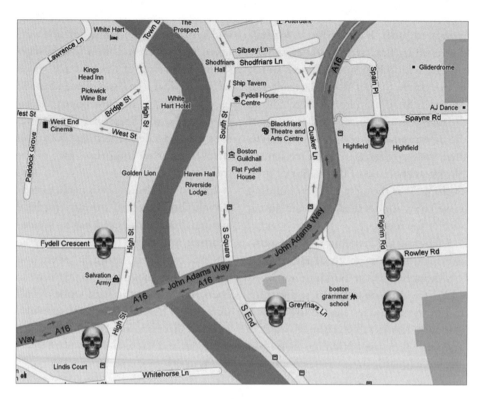

Map of Boston showing locations where medieval archeological digs uncovered tombs and skulls, thought to be linked to the 4 friaries and adjacent cemeteries that occupied a section of land to the east side of the river and small section to the west of the river during the medieval period, until religious reform in the mid-sixteenth century under the reign of King Henry VIII. (Map Data © 2012 Google, Phil King)

Paranormal Activity

The unusual events at Blackfriars first began during the period of renovation work and development of the theatre in the early 1960s, when staff member Margaret was approached by a mysterious monk and told 'Don't go into the theatre yet, because it is not ready'. This is not the only encounter that Margaret had with the ghostly monk; she apparently saw him on several other occasions – mostly on the stage in the theatre. Over the years the monk has been seen by numerous other people. He usually walks across the back of the stage and has apparently been captured in a photograph in that area during a night

vigil conducted by Midland Paranormal investigation team. The photograph was taken on the back wall to the right of the stage and appears to show a ghostly figure. The wall in question has a disused tunnel behind it, where victims of the plague were piled up during the Black Death (1348-1350), which decimated the population of Boston by approximately 30 per cent.

Sightings of the monk are not the only unexplained phenomenon to occur in this part of the building; there have been many instances over the years of objects going missing or being moved and light switches and equipment being turned on and off. A ghostly cat has been seen

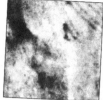

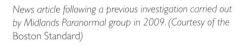

News article following a previous investigation carried out by Midlands Paranormal group in 2009. (Courtesy of the Boston Standard)

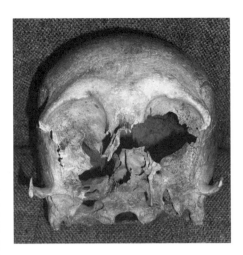

This skull was found beneath the foundations of Blackfriars during renovation works during the early 1960s. It is thought to belong to either a plague victim, or possibly a monk who may have perished in the fire of 1288. (Author's own photo)

walking across the piano and it has also been rumoured that an unknown entity hides sharp objects such as knives under the stage.

While the theatre itself is often said to be the most haunted part of the building, the unusual occurrences are by no means confined to that area. When I visited the theatre to interview the Director of Blackfriars, Mike Raymond, he told me of a ghostly figure that he himself had seen. At the time he was upstairs in one of the upper rooms showing his family around. First to enter the room, in his peripheral vision he saw a black figure running through that room and into the next. He chased after what he believed to be an intruder, as no one else was supposed to be in the building –

however, upon reaching the next room, the figure had vanished. The only way out of that room would have been an elevator (which there was no time to use) or back past Mike and his family. This experience left them all completely baffled, as not only did the mysterious figure vanish with no trace, but there had been no sounds to accompany the footsteps – something that had not occurred to them in the momentary instant of the event taking place. In fact, it had all occurred so quickly that there had been no time to notice any details about the dark figure, such as gender or clothing. Mike was so adamant of his sighting, however, that he had the whole building searched, determined to find a rational explanation for what he had seen. Although he was not able to come up with any explanation at all, his sighting was eventually validated by a further sighting of this mysterious figure elsewhere in the building by a colleague when someone was 'followed' into the print room downstairs, adjacent to the foyer, by what was described as a 'dark figure'. The foyer is also reputedly haunted by the ghost of a little boy.

Another area said to be haunted is the storage room beneath the stage. Several people have entered that room, only to feel an uncomfortable and oppressive atmosphere. In fact, one man is believed to have been possessed, or overcome, by an entity one night when he uncharacteristically began shouting 'Get out! get out! get out!' in an angry tone while down there. This experience caused the very frightened man to run from the building. The negativity in this room is believed to centre on the old projector in there, which once belonged to the Houses of Parliament. It is rumoured that the angry spirit, described as wearing 1960s style clothing, was once the projectionist and is very possessive of the object. It has been said that he travelled to Blackfriars with his projector and now does not want anyone else to be in the room with it.

Finally, for volunteers of Blackfriars, it would seem that even when they are not at the theatre they can still be affected by the paranormal activity going on within its thirteenth-century walls. The building alarm is frequently set off for no apparent reason, each time resulting in a volunteer having to attend the site and reset it – perhaps not the most popular of tasks given that this can occur in the middle of the night!

During my initial visit to Blackfriars to meet with Mike, I had my voice recorder running in order to capture my interview with him and, upon playing back the audio, I could hear a couple of strange anomalies in the sound that were not audible to me at the time of my visit. Firstly, whilst walking around the stage area of the theatre a male voice is heard saying 'Get out!'. This was not pleasant

to hear back, and I could not help but wonder whether this could be the infamous angry projectionist beneath the stage expressing his characteristic disapproval at my presence above. A further voice was recorded in a room upstairs – it was that of a female who seemed to be saying 'Help me'.

Having heard the many testimonies of paranormal activity associated with Blackfriars, seen unexplainable anomalies captured in photographs and heard my own EVPs captured on my initial visit, I was really excited about returning to Blackfriars with the 13 Paranormal investigation team a few weeks later to conduct an investigation.

Blackfriars Investigation – 4 August 2012

Present: Gemma King, Dean Grant, Chloe Watts, Stephanie Watson, Pete Creasy and Dan Watts (cameraman)

I began the investigation by setting out some trigger objects to encourage any resident spirits to engage with the team. These were as follows:

Marbles (foyer): I had heard speculation that the ghost of a little boy had been seen in the foyer so I introduced myself and left some marbles – on marked paper – for him to play with.

Knife (on the stage): It has been rumoured for many years that a mysterious entity hides sharp objects underneath the stage – although Theatre Director Mike was sceptical about this alleged phenomenon, having never witnessed it himself.

Religious Cross (on the stage): Given that the site was once occupied by friars and also that a ghostly monk has been photographed on the premises, I placed a cross on the stage in attempt to connect with any friars that may be resident in the building.

Séance

The team sat around a table in the upper room to begin a séance, opened by me. Audio recorders were also set up. When inviting the spirit energies to come forward, one of the KII meters on the table became very active, flickering all the way up to red. We heard tapping sounds in the room and also what sounded like shuffling feet at one stage – however the glass itself did not move and we therefore decided, after a short break, to move the séance downstairs to the theatre stage.

Regrettably we were still unable to engage with the spirit entities via the séance and the glass remained uncharacteristically still. I felt this was extremely unusual given that, in the many séances I have conducted over the years, I have never known the glass to remain motionless.

Table Tipping

Following the attempted séance, Dean produced his tipping table to see if any of the spirits would be able to communicate through that. It is a small table, approximately waist height and 1 foot square. It has one central leg down the centre and bracket style feet pointing outwards at the bottom. The idea is that a person places a finger on each corner, and any spirits that would like to communicate can do so by using our energy to rock the table. 13 Paranormal have previously had much success using this communication tool. Again, however, there was no movement and we decided to begin the vigils.

Orb anomaly captured in this photograph. It is visible to the right of Megan in the foyer. (Author's own photo)

Vigils

The first vigil was held in the projector room beneath the stage. An orb anomaly was captured next to the projector and whilst talking to any resident spirit energies, one investigator, sitting in the chair next to the projector, suddenly became overwhelmed by a sad feeling and became teary. At the same time, the EMF detector had become very active, lighting up all the way to red.

A short vigil was held in the studio on the top floor although nothing unusual occurred during that time and no activity was recorded on the EMF detector.

I spent some time in the foyer inviting any resident spirit energies to come forward and there was some EMF activity – also, a large white orb was captured on my camera.

The final vigil took place in the theatre, where many white orb anomalies, some very large, were captured on camera. A loud noise was also heard emanating from the back of the theatre in a production room. Upon entering the room to investigate the noise, Dean was photographed and a large white orb was visible by his head.

Conclusion and evidence

With regard to EVP recordings, there were five sound anomalies that were picked up in total. In addition to the voices I had recorded during my pre-investigation visit with Mike, sounds were recorded during the investigation. I had left an audio recorder running in the upper studio during the séance, and amongst all the tapping sounds we heard whilst inviting the spirits to move the glass, a voice was captured on the recorder saying 'Steph' – presumably referring to Steph on our team.

During our break from the séance in the upper studio, I had left the voice recorder running, and at a time when no one was in the room, a loud sound was recorded comparable to a chair dragging on the floor.

In addition to these sounds I heard faint voices on numerous occasions throughout the audio recording – most notably on and beneath the stage. However, the voices were so faint and distorted that I was not able to clearly decipher any one voice or word, and so I cannot categorise them as EVP recordings.

Many orbs were captured on camera, some very large. This, alongside the (at times) responsive EMF activity and the inexplicable sounds such as tapping and shuffling in the upper room led us to the conclusion that we were not alone. That said, in terms of investigating, it was unfortunate that Blackfriars was somewhat quiet on the night that the team visited. None of the trigger objects were moved and the séance did not provide us with any insight into the identity of the resident spirits.

Based on the testimonies of activity alone, I am in no doubt that Blackfriars is haunted and I hope to visit there to investigate again at some stage in the future. However, it is perhaps possible that the spirits residing there would prefer their identity to remain a mystery.

3

THE GLIDERDROME

The Gliderdrome has been in the Malkinson family for around 70 years, and its existence as an entertainment centre can be traced back to 1939, when it functioned as an open-air skating rink. Around this time it also became a venue for dancing, and during the Second World War the decision was made to transform the area into an enclosed building. Throughout the war years, local bands would frequently provide entertainment for dance nights, attracting the local community and military forces.

The investigation team setting up.

In 1959, however, the building was gutted by fire and had to be completely rebuilt. The Malkinsons opted to extend the existing premises, and added another function hall. This came to be known as the Starlight Room, and played host to sell-out concerts by big-name stars Tina Turner, Elton John, Marc Bolan and Jimmy Hendrix throughout the 1960s and '70s.

During construction of the Starlight Room, a startling discovery was made by contractors when digging up the floor. Ten bodies were uncovered – two in lead coffins and eight without

Sir Elton John and lyricist Bernie Taupin on their visit to the Gliderdrome in February 1973. (Picture courtesy of Andrew Malkinson)

coffins. The human remains are thought to date back to medieval times, when the land was used as a cemetery. This area of land is also a stone's throw from what would once have been the Dominican Friary – one of four monasteries that were established along that stretch of the River Witham – it is thought that the human remains beneath the Starlight Room may be those of monks.

In 1973 the Starlight Room closed for business, and the only part of the building still in regular use is the former skating rink and dance hall, which is now a bingo hall. There has been speculation of the venue re-opening its doors as a music venue once again in the future, but taking into consideration the history of the site, the tragic events of the

A proud moment for the Glider in January 1972, when Marc Bolan & T. Rex played at the venue. Admission was just 60p at the door! (Photo courtesy of Andrew Malkinson)

fire that destroyed the Dominican friary in 1281 and the fact that large parts of the building have been unoccupied for many years, it is perhaps no surprise that it has lent itself to ghost manifestation.

The first strange occurrence was witnessed by the owners, Andrew and Chris Malkinson, around 2009. They were standing in the office when they suddenly saw and felt the large heavy wooden table in the centre of the room jolt and move to one side, towards another desk in the room. The movement of the table was so vigorous that it caused the table to crash into a nearby office chair, which in turn, lunged forward and hit the desk in front of it. Andrew and Chris were left shocked when this happened, given the sheer weight of the table and the fact that neither of them had been standing anywhere near it at the time. Another inexplicable event occurred in the form of a photograph taken by Andrew in the storage area adjacent to the bingo hall – a smoky, ghostly-looking mist was captured in the photo and there was nothing nearby at the time that could have caused it.

Upon becoming aware of these mysterious occurrences, and in the knowledge that bodies were buried beneath the site, Team Manager Dean Grant from Paranormal 13 was keen for his group to carry out a full investigation of the premises using their specialist equipment and techniques to see if they could uncover any further paranormal phenomena, contact any entities that may be present, shed some light on who was responsible for the incident involving the table and maybe even capture some evidence of spirit communication on their equipment. Numerous investigations have now been carried out at the Gliderdrome by Dean and his team, and they have man-aged to record and experience a significant number of inexplicable events which leave them in no doubt whatsoever that the building is indeed haunted. These events include:

- Loud bangs in response to questions being asked
- Investigators being touched
- Furniture being moved/dragged
- Flashes of light
- Extreme temperature fluctuations
- An apparition figure seen on the balcony of the Starlight Room – at the same time as the KII meter displayed inexplicably high readings. Photos were taken at the time of this event and one shows a ghostly mist, thought to contain the image of a bearded man. An EVP was also captured on the audio at this time of a voice saying 'don't go there'; at that moment the investigation team were heading up to the balcony, to the exact spot where the apparition had been seen.

On one occasion, the team conducted an experiment whereby they played music then asked the spirits if they liked it. This proved to be very successful, with a female voice heard saying 'yes' and even the sound of someone snoring recorded on audio! The best part of this experiment, however, was the eerie white mist captured on DVR floating towards the stage while a song by Adele was being played.

When I heard about the experiences of Dean's team and the owners of the Gliderdrome, I was keen to meet them on location to conduct another investigation to see if we could uncover any further evidence of paranormal activity and spirit communication.

Gliderdrome Investigation – 25 February 2012

Present: Dean Grant (Team Leader), Adrian Fuller (Medium), Stephanie Watson (Investigator), Steve Virgo (Deputy Team Manager), Gemma King (Investigator).
Plus two guests invited by Dean, Storme and Chris Buttree

The evening began at 10 p.m. in the office, where we all gathered and planned the vigils for the night. We arranged it so that we would not all be investigating particular rooms at once, as firstly this can lend itself to noise contamination; secondly, if members of different groups have the same experience in a certain area, it can be really good validation; and finally, there is the potential to capture more evidence during investigations if the team breaks down into smaller groups. Dean gave me a tour of the building, starting in the bingo hall, and I took the opportunity to introduce myself to any spirits present. I invited them to come and say hello, explaining that I may not be able to hear their voices now, but they could be picked up by my voice recorder so I would be able to listen to their messages later. We started to take some photographs to see if any anomalies would be captured and it did not take long for a bright white orb to appear on Dean's camera.

As we walked through to the Starlight Room, I noticed a very discernible difference in the temperature, in that it was a lot colder than everywhere else. Dean explained that as the Starlight Room is never used anymore, it is no longer heated, so on occasions during investigations when they hear loud bangs around the room in response to questions, they know it cannot be attributed to the central heating system cooling down and is more likely to be paranormal.

This seems especially likely, considering that the Starlight Room has always been the most active area of the building with regard to experiences of the investigation team members on previous visits.

As before, upon entering the Starlight Room, I introduced myself to any spirits present and silently stood next to Dean in complete darkness. Opening all our senses, we invited any resident spirits to come forward and speak to us during our visit. While not deeply spiritually sensitive, Dean commented that he felt a sense of intrigue from the spirits associated with my presence. As before, I spoke to them and explained that their voices could be picked up by my voice recorder. All of a sudden there was a drop in temperature and I could see my breath. We heard a distinct creaky 'clomp' in front of us, which sounded like a random footstep.

In a later vigil with other team members in the Starlight Room, Dean referred back to his previous experiment in which he had played out music by different artists and asked whether the resident spirits enjoyed it. This time, he asked if anyone wanted to listen to Example. At this point a bang was heard right behind him at floor level. It sounded as though someone had dropped a stone next to him on the floor (although there was no stone or other object visible). The team explained that the most common phenomenon that they encounter in general at the Gliderdrome seems to be banging and tapping in response to questions, and I did notice this myself during the investigation, although they did also say that something different happens every time they investigate. On the vigil in the Starlight Room, Adrian and I could smell pipe smoke at one stage. This smell seemed to follow us to other parts of the building, periodically becoming quite potent.

As we left the Starlight Room we progressed through a corridor to an old disused lounge and bar area, where Dean told me of an experience he'd had on a previous investigation. Along that corridor there is a double swing door, and Dean recalled that on one occasion when he had been about to push the door open, an inexplicable force from the other side seemed to pull it, resulting in it coming right out of his hand. Many people have felt an oppressive sensation in that area, and on previous investigations the team have also noted the batteries in their equipment mysteriously becoming drained of power. The medium, Adrian, has previously sensed negativity in that area and during the two separate vigils on the night that I investigated with Paranormal 13, one person from each of the groups reported chest pains and a feeling of nausea.

This door adjacent to the Starlight Room was physically pulled from the hands of investigator Dean on one of their previous investigation nights at the venue. (Author's own photo)

Following that vigil, the whole team united for a second attempt in the bingo hall. As we sat together at adjoining tables in the centre of the hall, the pitch blackness of such a vast space meant that we could not see all the way to the edges of the room. We invited any spirits present to come and communicate with us, whether through banging on an object, talking to us or lighting up our EMF detectors. Our time in the bingo hall seemed quieter than the team had encountered on previous investigations, although my camera was picking up orb anomalies.

Before too long, however, we began to hear knocking sounds in response to questions and Adrian picked up on the presence of two spirits in the bingo hall – one was a lady called Gladdis, the other a gentleman called Albert. Gladdis communicated that she had once been a cleaner on the premises and now liked to sing to keep the energy in the building positive. Albert said that he had been an event organiser when the bingo hall was a skating rink and dance hall.

It was at this point that the most shocking event occurred. The table occupied by myself and Dean suddenly jolted to one side, as though someone on an adjoining table had clumsily stood up, knocking into ours. Also, when Dean invited the spirits to have a game of bingo, we heard the sound of one of the chairs either flipping up or down, as though someone in one of the distant seats was either getting up or sitting down.

For the final part of the investigation, Dean played music into the Starlight Room to see if we could prompt a response from any resident spirits, such as the eerie floating mist that had been captured on video floating towards the stage on a previous investigation.

The team have a short break and compare photographs in the office. The table where we are all gathered is the one that moved, all on its own, a couple of years prior to the time of writing this book – an experience that left owners Andrew and Chris Malkinson completely baffled. (Author's own photo)

Given that we were investigating on the anniversary of the concert by The Who in 1966, Dean opted to play their music. Throughout the songs, we captured a lot of bright orb anomalies in our photographs, and after the music had been played we could hear knocking sounds coming from the dressing room area at the back of the stage.

Upon closing the investigation, all that remained was to review the audio and video footage to see if any evidence of paranormal activity had been captured.

EVP

Several disembodied voices were captured on my audio voice recorder and sadly, not all were decipherable but the following audio events were picked up:

Stephanie entered the office and noted that there was some money on the floor – at this point, a disembodied voice is heard saying 'fell off of the table'.

Whilst in the office, I questioned whether the spirit that moved Chris and Andrew's table was present – a voice was recorded in response (although I have struggled to decipher exactly what is being said.) In the bingo hall, a knock is heard – I then say, 'they're probably telling me to wake up because I'm really tired!' A voice responds 'YES'.

Upon being invited to play bingo, a voice is heard on the audio saying 'I want a turn, thank you'.

In the bingo hall a woman's voice was recorded saying 'M-hm' as if in agreement to something – several investigators actually heard this during the vigil itself.

In the bingo hall, Dean invited the spirits to slide the plastic bingo board off the table – a voice was recorded saying 'OK'.

Dean and his team frequently return to the Gliderdrome, often taking guests with them. Given that they have experienced many active investigation nights there, it is likely that it will remain one of their regular 'haunts' in the years to come.

4

CHURCH KEY STUDIO, 28-30 CHURCH STREET

Church Key Studio. (Author's own photo)

With an estimated construction date of 1520, this characteristic Grade II listed building adjacent to the St Boltoph's church has been a tourist attraction for many years. In its 500-year history it has seen many different uses and occupants including a Thai restaurant, a body piercing shop, and a photographer's studio. The ancient weathered sign on the outside wall that reads 'Church Key Studio' is believed to date back to a time when the church keys were kept there, raising the possibility that the building may at one stage, amidst its long history of owners and functions, have had a connection with the church.

Of all the residents that have occupied this building over the years, however, the most talked-about is the infamous Sarah Preston. A local folk tale tells the horrific story of her infidelity, guilt and suicide. The tragic tale is set in 1585, when Sarah and her husband, a businessman, had recently bought the building as their marital home.

With her husband frequently travelling in his line of business, Sarah often found herself alone in the house for many days at a time. It was said that on many occasions while her husband was away she was unfaithful, inviting would-be lovers to the house to spend nights with her. It is said that on one fateful night, Sarah invited a sailor to her home. She spent the night with him, and it was then discovered that he had brought the plague to town with him, which subsequently caused the death of 460 Bostonians.

Church Key Studio, c. 1850 – this picture shows no signs of its Tudor beginnings, which were restored in the following century. (Photo courtesy of Sandra Sales)

With everyone blaming her for bringing the plague to Boston, Sarah Preston became racked with guilt and ran towards St Boltoph's church with hysterical cries of 'pestilence!' She then climbed the church tower and threw herself off the top, falling to her death.

It is now said that during the autumn months, her disembodied cries of 'pestilence!' can sometimes be heard around the church. Her ghostly apparition has also been seen jumping from the top of the tower and disappearing before hitting the ground.

When the plague swept through Boston, victims of the terrible disease had to be buried immediately upon death due to the highly contagious nature of the illness. Tragically, given that one of the symptoms of the plague was the sufferer falling into a coma, there were some cases where people were presumed to be dead, but were in fact mistakenly buried alive. There were cases of mourners standing at the graveside looking on in horror as hands of plague victims they had buried appeared through the soil of their freshly covered graves. Many bodies were buried in an area close to the church, near to the Church Key Studio building. One cannot help but wonder how many premature burials occurred on this site, never to be discovered.

'Spooky' Tales From A Resident Family

In 1990, Church Key Studio was purchased by Mr and Mrs Sales with a view to turning the building into an esoteric shop and tea room. This process was not an immediate one, as Ian and Sandra Sales owned many different shops at the time and were busy with other commitments. However, the upstairs of the building was sometimes rented out as accommodation throughout the 1990s. Their daughter Jenny also took up residence, living there on and off by herself throughout this period.

During the time spent living there she began hearing what she describes as gentle harpsichord music – a distant and very pleasant sound – but she was never able to trace the source of it. There were no neighbours, and she knew it was not coming from the church. In fact, it seemed to be emanating from the upstairs front room; a large room at the top of the stairs, which overlooks the river. This was to be the first of many notable events, most of which were attributed to the presence of a mischievous spirit.

Jenny's parents eventually moved in and established a tea shop on the ground floor. They planned to convert the large upstairs room into a shop, selling crystals, tarot cards, distinguished ornamental pieces and unique gifts.

Being a builder, Ian was keen to begin the process of transforming the room and worked into the night clearing it out. At approximately 1.30 a.m. he went into the bedroom and said to Sandra 'I don't want to work in there anymore.' Sandra asked why, and he reported that he felt a 'spooky' oppressive feeling whilst working, along with a feeling of being very cold. In addition, all of the lights had gone out in that room. Sandra confirmed that she had not turned the lights off but upon examination, they found that the light bulbs from that room had been removed from their fittings and placed on a table. This was baffling to the family, as they all knew no one had done it.

The staircase, where many people have felt the presence of someone following them. There were several orb anomalies captured in this picture; more are visible on the website version.

The strange activity continued, and over the years the most common phenomenon seemed to be that objects would be taken by an unknown entity, never to be seen again. Amongst the family this became a bit of a running joke at the expense of poor Ian, a tough-as-nails Yorkshireman typically unrattled by any ghostly tale, who seemed to fall foul of the mischievous female spirit most often.

He frequently had items completely vanish, and it would never be old items – it would always be something new and valuable that he was particularly proud of. Mrs Sales recalled that he once spent over £200 on a new pair of glasses, and upon putting them down in a familiar place, they mysteriously vanished. The house was turned upside down in the search for them but they were never found. This also happened with many precious items, including a ring that Sandra had bought him for an anniversary. Despite Ian seemingly being the main target of this phenomenon, he was by no means the only victim. A member of staff from the café once had a much treasured picture taken and, on one occasion, Mrs Sales herself had a legal document taken. Everyone carried out a meticulous search for this document because of the important and personal nature of the content – however, it was never found, and she had to pay another £50 to have a duplicate made. The story did not end there, however; once she had paid to have the new document drawn up, the original one inexplicably reappeared on the shop counter.

Often, upon visiting the tea shop, children would say to their parents 'Isn't it spooky in here!'

It was from here that the name of the new upstairs gift shop originated – 'Spookys'. When the shop was up and running, quite a few psychics would note the presence of a female spirit upstairs in the front room. They would say 'Did you know that there is a lady sitting in the corner of the room smiling at you?' the family would simply acknowledge this, completely unsurprised. The lady is described as wearing a grey dress and bonnet, and it is said that she sits in that corner, smiling at people in the room.

Although the family never actually saw this lady, there was one occasion when Jenny believes that she may have heard her presence. Late one night, whilst locking up the building, she heard a female laughing in the room. She tried to debunk this sound as the novelty mirrors, sold upstairs, that made a laughing

The upstairs room at the centre of the activity, showing the author's impression of the corner where the ghostly female has been seen sitting, smiling at people. (Photo courtesy of Phil King)

sound when someone stood in front of them. However, upon checking the two mirrors that they had in stock at the time, neither had batteries in. There was no other explanation for this laughter and Jenny was left truly bewildered.

During my communications with the Sales family about the strange occurrences at Church Key Studio over their twenty year period of ownership, it was very clear that the spirit presence in the building is not a negative one and they never felt scared or uncomfortable by anything that happened. The only exception to this is the staircase leading to the large front room; many people have felt as though someone is following them when walking up and down those stairs. Jenny recalled during my interview with her that the stairs were the only part of the building where she sometimes felt particularly uncomfortable.

5

HAUNTED PUBS OF BOSTON

The Britannia, Church Street

The Britannia. (Author's own photo)

The current landlady of the Britannia had only been in residence at the pub for a few months when I interviewed her in connection with paranormal activity. However, in that interview, landlady Vicky Ross and landlord Mick Norman explained that during their short period of occupancy they have experienced quite a few spooky and inexplicable events.

The first thing they noticed was that on many occasions, midway through the afternoon, the gas to the beer supply would suddenly cut off. Upon going down to the cellar to investigate, they would find that not just one, but all three of the gas taps had been turned off. At the time of my interview, this had occurred in excess of fifteen times and the staff were still completely baffled by it.

On another occasion the landlord was hoovering the ladies' toilets. Upon realising he had left one of the attachments on a table in the bar lounge, he temporarily switched the hoover off to go and fetch it – but just as he was picking it up, the hoover inexplicably switched itself on again with no one near it. Also in the ladies' toilets, a strange chalk-like mark appeared on the floor which looked a bit like a letter 'C'. It had not been there all night but was noticed by Vicky and Mick upon closing up. Many attempts, with various different cleaning products, were made to clean it off but all proved fruitless. In trying to work out what had caused the stain to appear on the floor, staff had considered the possibility of it being made by dirt trapped underneath the door. However, this suggestion was quickly ruled out by the fact that the door does not swing both ways and therefore cannot reach far enough to cover the whole stain line. The mystery of the stain did not end here; they came down the following morning to find that the stain had completely vanished without a trace.

Another strange and unexplained sighting was that of a man sitting in the corner of pub – this would not usually be a strange sight; however, the image was spotted on a CCTV screen at a time when no one was there! Having been watching the image on the screen from upstairs for several minutes, Mick went downstairs to investigate but there was no one to be seen. Vicky also explained that they have often heard the sounds of doors opening and closing downstairs when they are in bed at night. Despite the sounds, no doors have actually been opened and it remains a mystery where the sounds emanate from, as the neighbouring building is always unoccupied at the time when the noises are heard.

As well as speaking with Vicky and Mick about their time in the pub I also spoke with Zoe, who used to work at the

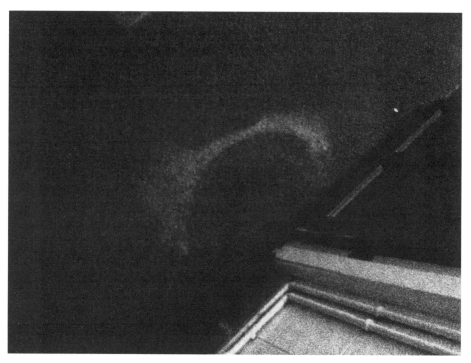

The chalk-like mark that mysteriously appeared on the floor of the ladies' toilets. As the picture illustrates, the door stops considerably short of the white mark, so could not have created it. (Photo courtesy of Vicky Ross)

The shelf that glasses inexplicably flew from.

Britannia when the previous occupants were in residence. Zoe recalled that when working in the kitchen she frequently experienced utensils and other objects going missing. She initially shrugged it off but eventually mentioned it to another member of staff, who responded, 'that'll be the ghost'. It transpired that the other employees were already aware of the unusual occurrences, having had many experiences of their own.

Zoe recalled that she used to lock up; on one occasion she saw a black figure – believed to be male – standing upstairs in the living room, which at that time was used as an office.

The most recent activity noted in the pub was that of glasses and bottles flying from the shelves behind the bar and landing several feet away. Disturbed by this, and trying to find a cause in order to prevent such a dangerous occurrence from happening again, Mick examined the shelves and tried to re-enact what was happening but was left completely puzzled. He and Vicky quickly reached the conclusion that according to the laws of gravity it was physically impossible for the glasses to fall in the way that they were without being assisted.

Mick finally lost patience one day when an object suddenly flew from a shelf behind the bar, missing him by inches. He assertively told the entity to go away, and since then no activity has been reported at all.

On a personal note, I always recommend that people use this technique to try and expel an unwanted spirit presence as it has been proven to work in many cases – though sadly not all.

The Stump and Candle, Market Place

Locals have speculated that one of the spirits connected to this pub could be that of John Foxe, a sixteenth-century author, historian and influential campaigner against religious persecution, as this building was his birth place. His controversial work, *The Book of Martyrs*, which told of the pain and suffering of Protestants in previous centuries was widely acclaimed and was thought to have influenced public opinion about the Catholic Church for centuries to come.

An apparition of a man in period costume has been seen by a customer in this pub and other unexplained phenomena include an unknown entity that touches the bottoms of people working in the kitchen, and a woman that has been seen standing in the middle window at the front of the pub.

Goodbarns Yard, Wormgate

Located in very close proximity to the spectacular and notable St Boltophs Church (The Stump), Goodbarns Yard in itself (now a Grade II listed building) has an extensive history, with the original front section dating back approximately 470 years. Initially the building was a grammar school run by the town guilds, and part of what we now know as the pub (the rear elevation) used to form part of a different street with a row of houses. Also, the streets that surround Garbarns Yard were not always the pleasant and characteristic streets that we see today – in previous centuries, prostitutes would traverse the cobbles outside the building. The extension and development of the pub in more recent years has meant that centuries of eventful history on the streets and from buildings previously on that site have now become part of the pub.

The Stump & Candle (Author's own photo); and John Foxe. (Courtesy of Billy Jenthorn)

Goodbarns Yard. (Author's own photo)

The bar, where male apparitions and floating orbs have been seen. (Author's own photo)

The current landlady has reported frequently seeing orbs of light floating around the pub, particularly in the restaurant area. An apparition of a gentleman wearing a blue shirt has been seen walking through the pub, and a ghostly cat has also been spotted walking through the pub in the area that would have previously been a street.

The living quarters of the pub upstairs are part of the original building, and the current landlady recalls that she experiences unusual phenomena such as unexplainable sounds and cold spots. On one occasion two staff members, alone in the building, were carrying chairs upstairs. They each left a chair in one of the first floor rooms and were stunned to find a few minutes later that one of the chairs had been moved out of the room and into the hallway by an unknown entity.

Despite the occasional ghostly visitors to Goodbarns Yard, the current owner has never experienced or sensed anything negative, and none of the phenomena experienced has ever caused any problems.

The Red Cow Inn, Fishtoft

Once sectioned off and used partly as a mortuary, this historic pub on Gaysfield Road, Fishtoft, has been the setting of some strange sights and sounds, noted by the current owner Bonnie and her husband (formerly a non-believer in most things paranormal) during their time in residence.

Bonnie explained that on several occasions, her husband has sat at the bar after closing time and has suddenly become aware of children in Victorian

The Red Cow Inn. (Author's own photo)

clothing running through the toilet doorway and out into the pub. Over the years he has apparently seen four different children ranging in age from approximately three to ten years old. It was not possible to see facial detail, and the image was not there for long, but it was long enough for there to be no question that the apparitions were not a figment of his imagination. The visual spectacle of the children has never been accompanied by any sound or direct communication, but their movement is playful and happy and they never seem to be in any distress.

In another incident, Bonnie recalls hearing a noise which she believes may have saved her child from a serious accident. She was working in the upstairs kitchen, while her young son was in his bedroom with a friend who had come to play with him.

The bar area, where children in period clothing were seen playfully running. (Author's own photo)

Suddenly the stair gate began to rattle vigorously; upon coming to investigate the noise, Bonnie found that the two boys were still happily playing in the bedroom where they had been for quite some time, but the stair gate was wide open and had obviously been left open by mistake. Bonnie did not know who had been rattling it and was baffled by this, as there was no one else around, but likes the thought that it may have been one of their resident spirits trying to warn her of the danger.

While Bonnie and her husband are in no doubt that their pub is haunted by residents of the past, there is nothing negative about the presences and the atmosphere is always a happy one.

The Castle Inn, Haltoft End, Freiston

Jim and Cath have been managers of The Castle Inn for fifteen years. During that time, some strange phenomena have been experienced by their staff, and by long term visitor Christine Allen, who has been the life and soul of the pub and restaurant for forty-one years.

The most common phenomenon experienced by staff relates to objects moving by themselves. On occasion, when they reach for it moments later they discover it has disappeared. After a long laborious search, the item will reappear where they last saw it. Initially dismissing these occurrences as just bouts of forgetfulness, the staff now believe there may be a more ghostly explanation given the other phenomena that takes place in the building. In addition to the moving objects, items of furniture are sometimes mysteriously moved, both in the restaurant and kitchen area of the building. On one occasion, Cath had very carefully stacked some pots in the kitchen and upon leaving the room and ascending the stairs suddenly heard a big crash – the pots had fallen and were scattered everywhere. To this day, Cath is adamant that they had been stacked in such a way that there is no way they could have fallen on their own – and it is not just the pots in the kitchen that have been tampered with. On another occasion a chair was inexplicably moved in the kitchen; Cath had tucked all the chairs under the kitchen table and then left the room to go upstairs. When she was halfway up the stairs she had heard the sound of a chair dragging on the floor, and upon coming back downstairs to look, was shocked to find that one of the kitchen chairs had been pulled away from the table – seemingly by nobody!

When I was talking with Cath, she recalled that the mystery of the moving chair in the kitchen was by no means an isolated incident, in the sense that an unexplainable event also occurred in the restaurant area, on a much larger scale, again involving chairs. She first explained how particular they are when closing up at night about the chairs all being squarely tucked under the tables, and recalled that on the night of the incident she had witnessed a staff member tucking away the chairs properly and had been satisfied that everything was left as it should be when they went to bed.

However, upon coming downstairs the following morning she was stunned to note that many of the chairs had been pulled away from the tables and turned to a slight angle. No explanation could be found for this at all, and to this day they can only put it down to their resident ghost, who they affectionately speak of as a 'him'.

The Castle Inn. (Author's own photo)

One staff member, Natalie Harrison, recalled that she feels very uneasy when going to clean the toilet area of the building because she will often get a sense that she is being watched – she has seen a black shadow figure dash past her on several occasions. The figure is usually accompanied by a swift drop in temperature. Staff will also often feel a sensation of someone standing behind them looking over their shoulder – again, accompanied by a notable drop in temperature.

The identity of the mischievous spirit who likes to visit The Castle Inn is not known, though he is not considered to be unfriendly. In fact, Cath now speaks to him on some occasions – particularly when he has hidden something that she needs to use and she wants him to give it back!

Jolly Crispin, West Street

The history of the Jolly Crispin public house has been traced back to the 1800s, and records show that the building has always been a pub.

The Jolly Crispin. (Author's own photo)

Nigel Crowe has been running the Jolly Crispin for six years, and the staff have frequently noticed during this time that the beer gas cylinders in the cellar have mysteriously turned themselves off on a regular basis. Doing so involves physically turning the stiff taps into the 'off' position, and this is one reason why the strange phenomenon has baffled everyone.

One member of staff become so 'freaked out' by this that she placed rosary beads on them, and was amazed to find that this seemed to put a stop to the problem. However, by way of experiment, the staff removed the beads and were stunned to note that the cylinders once again began turning themselves off.

Since May 2012, the upstairs of the pub has been running as a bed and breakfast and one guest has noted sensations of a 'presence' in his room.

The history of the building is extensive and throughout its many years as a drinking house, there have been many occupants. It is even said that there was once a suicide on the premises.

The story is known of one particular gentleman who occupied the building throughout the late 1800s and early 1900s: William Woodcock. Known in his lifetime as an alcoholic, he drank himself to death on the premises in 1906. Records show that prior to his death he resided there with his first wife Mary Ann until her death in 1883, then his second wife Martha who is shown on census records from 1891. By the time that the census records were updated in 1901 he had married again and his third and final wife, Selina Julia, outlived him.

It is said that the ghost on the premises today is female, although no one has actually seen her. Is it possible that it is one of William Woodcock's wives?

Perhaps she is turning off the beer gas in an attempt to put a stop to the excessive consumption of alcohol that eventually killed her husband.

The Butchers Arms, Commonside, Old Leake

Brett and Kerry Copeland had only been running The Butchers Arms for one year when I visited them; however, they have already noticed strange occurrences during that time.

The first was late one evening, when the pub was almost empty. Brett was talking with the only two remaining customers at the bar when he became aware of a gentleman walking across the other end of the pub – from one end to the other. Ordinarily this would not be an unusual

sighting, but what *was* strange was that the gentleman emerged through the wall on the right-hand side of the pub and walked across to the left side of the pub, out of sight from where Brett was standing at the time. The place where the male apparition (dressed in relatively modern clothing) appeared used to be the main entrance to the building – and the area where he was heading was formerly the bar.

The renovation work which changed the pub's layout is thought to have taken place in the 1980s. Given that the apparition wears relatively modern clothing, it could be possible that a former customer who visited the pub sometime in the twentieth century is still visiting today. To me, this type of sighting would normally suggest a residual energy rather than an 'intelligent spirit'. Residual spirits will walk through

This picture shows the current pub layout –the brick columns on the right and left towards the back of the picture show the route taken by the male apparition as he emerged through the wall on the right (the location of former entrance which is now bricked up), and disappeared out of sight, heading towards what used to be the bar.

the original layout of a building, much as they did in life, and their routes are unaffected by building renovations. These ghostly sightings are the result of energy trapped in the masonry of a building and released at a later date.

Whilst further sightings of the ghostly gentleman walking that path that would support the concept of him being a residual energy, in the case of The Butchers Arms there has been another unusual phenomenon that suggests the presence of intelligent spirit in the building. Brett is particular about cleaning, and he vigorously maintains the same routine every day while doing so.

On a couple of occasions now, he has noted that when moves and replaces the heavy wicker chairs at one particular table, he will re-enter the room and find the same one pulled out again – some distance from the table. He shrugged it off the first time, but when it happened a second time he was really certain that he had put it back, because he had been very careful to do so. He is now extremely particular and jokes that he now keeps a close eye on those chairs every time he cleans, because he is sure that someone is moving them.

The Bricklayers Arms, Wainfleet Road, Old Leake

The Bricklayers Arms was formerly a brewery, and was built and run by brothers George and Samuel Horton. They were bricklayers by trade and construction of the brewery was completed in 1841. The 171-year-old building is most likely to have been constructed using bricks from the Wrangle brick pits, as George Horton owned them around that time.

For many years the building was occupied by members of the Horton family, including George himself and various servants and lodgers. The brewery was first listed as a beer retailer in 1868 in a Post Office Directory, and it remained in the Horton family until 1904 when George died. By this time it had ceased function as a brewery, as in 1901 the brewery had to close due to poor water supplies.

In 1905 the Bricklayers Arms was taken over by William Bush, who ran the pub until the 1920s. It has been a Batemans pub since at least 1917. Mrs Bateman supplied the porch on the front door of the pub, bringing it from her own house as it has a point to stop the devil landing on it

The Bricklayers Arms – 10 Commandments

1 When thirsty thou shalt come into my house and drink, but not to excess, then thou may live long in the land and enjoy thyself forever

2. Thou shall not take anything from me that is unjust, for I need all I have and more too.

3. Thou shall not expect too large glasses, nor filled too full, for we must pay our next rent

4. Thou shall not sing nor dance, only when the spirit is moved thee to do thy best.

5. Thou shall honour me and mine that thou mayest live long and see me again.

6. Thou shall not destroy nor break anything on my premises, else thou shall pay for double the value, thou shall not come to pay me in bad money, nor even say chalk or slate.

7. Thou shall call at my place daily; if unable to come we shall feel it an insult, unless thou send a substitute or apology.

8. Thou shall not abuse thy fellow bummers, nor cast base insinuations upon their character by hinting they cannot drink too much.

9. Neither shall thy take thy name of my goods in vain by calling my beer "slops" for I always keep the best brewed all, and am always at home to my friends.

10. Thou shall not so far forget their honourable position and high standard in the community as to ask the hotel keeper to treat them.

Notice: Will the lady and gentleman who stole two glasses on Saturday night, kindly hand their names over the counter, when they will be presented with four more to make up the half dozen.

This picture shows a recently re-written sheet, depicting the Ten Commandments of the pub. It thought to have been present on the wall for over a century. (Author's own photo)

– perhaps she was aware of unusual occurrences in the building in previous years!

The current owners of the pub, Brian and Trina Moreley, (plus their three children) had been resident for two years at the time I interviewed them. It was clear from our conversation, where I heard about their many eerie experiences during that time, that this pub was one of the most active I had come across in the area. In fact, the paranormal activity became notable in their first week of residence.

Firstly, the keys to the building went missing – they were very particular about where they kept them but on this occasion could not find them, which resulted in them having to leave the building unlocked overnight. After a thorough search of the building they were found in the conservatory, in a tool box with the lid closed. This remains a mystery, but was only the start of an escalating number of occurrences – not just involving movement of objects but in actual sightings of ghostly figures, as well as sounds and smells they could not explain.

The next occurrence came after closing one night, when Brian and his son were decorating the restaurant area. All of a sudden they became aware of the smell of horses, and this was closely followed by the sound of a horse neighing. The sound frightened them and seemed to come from outside the fire exit door. The pub's location is remote and there were no horses around, which left them completely baffled. Just as they were trying to make sense of what was going on, a small disco box situated in the restaurant suddenly shot across the room, with no apparent cause. Wine glasses that were set out on the tables also started making 'chinking' sounds as though being knocked together – impact between wine glasses was not possible as they were set out at individual placements with napkins inside and were not touching.

During my interview with Trina, she told me that almost every morning, when she comes downstairs, she discovers that one of the restaurant chairs has been moved back from the table, as though someone has pulled it out to sit down – and it is the same one every time. Trina is scrupulous about tucking all the chairs in when she closes up at night and cannot explain why one particular chair is frequently found to be out of place by the morning.

Local folklore tells the story of a girl who died on the premises, although there are two different versions of the story – some say that she died in the stable in an accident involving a horse and others say that she fell down the well to her death – the well and stables were located in what is now the restaurant area.

That said, there has also been activity experienced in the lounge area, and behind the bar itself – for example, whenever a new member of staff goes behind the bar to serve, items including bottles are thrown at them by an unknown entity.

Customers' drinks and items such as spectacles have inexplicably gone flying off tables. One customer has reported a ghostly male figure in a blue shirt walking up to the bar and vanishing.

There have also been other ghostly sightings – one was reported by Brian. He was locking up the pub one night, and having turned out most of the lights, called across to what he believed to be his adult son walking through the pub, asking him to fetch the keys. The pub was dark and as he called out, the male figure continued walking towards the restaurant. The figure then disappeared into the dark restaurant doorway and as Brian looked up and called out again, he realised that his son had been in the kitchen with Trina the whole time. The experience left Brian petrified.

It is not just Brian, Trina and their staff and customers that have been affected by the paranormal events taking place in the pub. Trina's six-year-old son has also reported an eerie sighting. He was standing in the pub area at the time and Trina was in the kitchen, preparing food. Suddenly his attention was drawn to the glass-panelled door leading to their private accommodation upstairs, as a male figure had appeared on the other side of the glass and was staring at him through the panels. He quickly went to fetch the barman as it is forbidden for visitors to go upstairs – but when the barman looked there was no trace of the male figure, and no one had either gone upstairs or left the building. Unbeknown to her son, the possibility of a ghostly male presence upstairs in the living quarters of the building had already occurred to Trina following a previous experience: she was lying in bed one night starting to doze, and she felt a man approach. He bent down and kissed her lips. It woke her up, but when she looked around there was no sign of her husband; and when she went downstairs and asked Brian if he had been upstairs, he confirmed that he had not. Trina was quite shocked by this as she knew she had not been dreaming, although she did not feel threatened by it. She has also experienced a sensation of someone pushing the panelled door when she tries to open it, as though someone is trying to stop her.

Their eldest son's girlfriend was once using one of the upstairs bathrooms when she had an experience that terrified her. While she was in the room, the door to the bathroom unlocked itself and the door swung open towards her. No one could have done this from the outside, and the experience left her so frightened that she now she refuses to go upstairs in the building.

On another occasion, a door locked by itself – Trina's six-year-old son walked into the conservatory and the door closed and locked behind him, trapping him inside. It was several minutes before he was found and he became very distressed. Another son has also had strange experiences in the building – he recalled getting up in the night to use the bathroom and, while in there, hearing footsteps walking up and down the landing outside

The bathroom door, which unbolted and swung open on its own. (Author's own photo)

A chair in the restaurant that is frequently found pulled out from the table. (Author's own photo)

the door. A further unexplained phenomenon occurred when Trina and Brian heard heavy banging on their flat roof when they had been sitting in the pub socialising with friends. They thought it may be burglars, and upon hearing the loud thuds, went to explore with torches, but they could not find any source for the noise.

Trina was once talking to a visitor, recalling how the unknown ghostly entity presses pause on her stereo – and while they were talking, as if on cue, the stereo paused itself!

Trina does not feel threatened by the activity that takes place, though she did admit that it does take her by surprise and some of her experiences make her feel slightly uncomfortable. She spoke of an occasion when she was upstairs in the bathroom and she could hear a dis-embodied child's voice calling 'Mummy, Mummy'. It was definitely not one of her children, and there was no other possible explanation for the sound. Other people that have been upstairs have also reported this ghostly voice.

A former cleaner of the pub, who considered herself to be sensitive to spirits, said that she sensed there were two spirit children – a boy and a girl – present in the building. She said that they kept turning off the hoover while she was using it. This revelation rang alarm bells with Trina when she was talking to the cleaner, as she herself had noted that her hoovers kept breaking. They broke every two-three months and replacements were costing her a lot of money. The cleaner also reported that she had sometimes seen the lights above the pool table swinging.

With so much activity going on at The Bricklayers Arms, the owners were keen to for me to investigate it to see if I could find out the identity of any spirits residing in the building. Given the frightening nature of some of the events that had been taking place, and in particular the fact that children reside there, I was keen to find answers for the family and maybe even find a solution that could minimise activity, as this has been achieved on other investigations. I also wanted to capture evidence of the activity taking place and ensure that any spirits residing in the building were happy, as help can be given to unhappy spirits and negative entities can be moved on. A date was therefore agreed for me to return, in order to carry out an investigation. Before I did return to investigate, however, Trina reported further unexplained activity – the chair had been pulled out again and a poppy had been left on it; more disembodied footsteps were heard upstairs and the hoover had broken again. This further fuelled my determination to find some answers through the investigation.

The Bricklayers Arms Investigation – Friday 23 November 2012

Present: Gemma King, Chloe Watts and Serena Watts (investigators), Den Watts (cameraman). Plus pub residents Brian and Trina and some of their close friends.

As with any investigation, the evening began setting up and taking base readings. I then placed trigger objects upstairs and downstairs; all toys as I suspected that there were spirit children resident in the building, based on the testimonies of activity. I wanted to engage with them and attract their attention, so I tried to find old toys that would interest them. One was a musical box with a dancing figure inside (which I wound up and left playing initially in the hope that it would attract any children present); there was also a cup and ball, a spinning top and a rag doll.

Upon placing the items out and drawing around them to mark their exact position I introduced myself to the children and invited them to play with the toys.

As I went downstairs having left some toys in the upper hall where children can often be heard, the sound of a child humming was picked up on the voice recorder which I had left next to where the toys had been placed, though of course I was not aware of this until I played back the audio afterwards.

I ensured that all WIFI-enabled devices and mobile phones were switched off then carried out an EMF sweep of the building. The most readings were being picked up downstairs, which I would expect as spirits do tend to follow people during investigations as they are curious about what you are doing, and children in particular often want to engage with you.

Many photographs were taken and very large orb anomalies were captured around the main pub area of the building – some appeared to be moving and looked like large beams of light. One in particular was taken by the pub owner himself just before my arrival, and appears to be coming down through the ceiling from upstairs. (The best photos will be uploaded to the book website where viewing will be clearest).

After an initial period of setting up and taking photographs and EMF readings, the group gathered around the séance board and I opened spirit communication as usual with a short protection prayer. It did not take long for the glass to begin gliding around the table. Communications were not aimed at any one individual, but I was able to ask questions and got some good responses – although they were quite nonsensical at times, given that the main spirits engaging with us were children, and the children that come through are not always able to spell out answers to questions. That said, they are always happy to interact with us on the board. We made contact with a little boy who gave his name as FRED. As you would expect, he had difficulty spelling on the board so I pointed to YES and NO on the board and reverted to using just those. Through that, we worked out that he had an older sister, and a twin brother. We then asked if his older sister (aged seven) would like to talk with us as I thought that she may find it easier to spell, and this might lead to more accurate information coming through. Sure enough, the seven-year-old girl appeared straight away. We started off with a game

The panelled door, with author's impression of the male figure seen by Trina's son. (Author's own photo)

to keep it fun and I placed four coins on the board. The children used the glass to knock off all the coins, which was lovely and something they said they liked doing (this event is viewable on my website).

We then asked the little girl to confirm her names and age –she gave her name as FAY, and said that she had passed away in 1864 aged seven from an illness. She gave one brother's name as FREDERICK but, sadly, we could not get the name of the other brother. She told us that they had all passed away through illness and also gave the names GEORGE and ELIZABETH as her parents. She also told us that a lady called HARRIET resides in the building and causes a lot of mischief. I asked if I could speak to Harriet, and she did come on to the board. I offered Harriet reassurances that we were not there to upset her or move her on, and that we were friends who merely want to preserve the history and memories of the beautiful building. She confirmed that it is her that interferes with the hoover and I empathised with her, apologising for the noise it makes but also stating that Trina and Brian really need to use it to keep the floor clean. I wondered if this would help her to understand and respect the needs of the current owners, I but knew that only time would tell whether that tactic had worked.

I thanked Harriet for coming to speak with us and closed the séance.

During the investigation, our attention was drawn to the musical dancing doll as the EMF detector had started vigorously flashing red next to this toy. I spoke to the children and invited them to play with it, and photographs were taken at this time, which showed orbs around my legs. (Footage of this event can be seen on the website).

The investigation ended at 2 a.m.

After The Investigation

Following the investigation there was much to do by way of trying to validate the names that had come through on the séance board, examining photographs and listening to the audio for anomalies.

Historical researcher Shirley Elrick carried out some extensive research into this location and was able to trace George and Elizabeth Horton in this building around the time given to us, which was 1864 (it was the 1861 and 1871 census records that validated their existence). They were also shown as having children, but sadly nothing further could be found in relation to them. The children remain a mystery as birth and death records do not show them either – and Fay was not a name that was commonly used at that time. It may have been short for something else; however, the research trail ran cold with regard to specific details about the children. That said, the fact that records show George, Elizabeth and Harriet Horton did exist and reside in the building at the time given is an excellent validation.

Overall this is a good result, and the investigation results are also insightful for the owners as they now know who is responsible for the activity and why it occurs. The little boy said that he liked to play with their son, who is of a similar age, and Harriet is friendly – she just likes to make her presence known. They also know that, contrary to previous rumours, the resident spirit of the little girl is not someone that fell down a well or had an accident in a stable – that may well have happened at some stage in history, but the particular spirit we were in communication with who likes to play in the building died from an illness.

It was nice to know that the spirits residing in the building are all happy and none were in need of help.

Having reviewed the audio evidence from the voice recorder upstairs there was just one anomaly found; it picked up the sound of a child humming next to the toys just after the moment that I had placed them on the floor.

With regard to the other voice recorder, there was a technical issue and it did not record anything, which remains a mystery as I can visualise that evening, turning it on and seeing the timer ticking! I did return to site at a later date and conduct some EVP work, but did not record any further anomalies.

Ye Olde Magnet Tavern, South Square

Ye Olde Magnet Tavern was originally constructed in the mid-eighteenth century and was a drinking house and inn for many years. For a short time during the twentieth century it was converted into four separate houses; however, in the mid to late twentieth century it was restored back to its original function as a pub and bed and breakfast.

The current landlady of the pub, Donna Lumley, resides there with her husband and four children and ever since taking up residence above the pub, has felt an eerie presence as though she is being watched. Furthermore, unexplainable incidents have occurred that have left her in no doubt that the customers in the pub and guests in her bed and breakfast are not the only visitors in the building.

In addition to feeling as though she is being watched, strange activity has been occurring in the pub – glasses have been known to fly off the shelves, and when one toilet is being used in the ladies' room, the other will inexplicably flush.

Furthermore, the balls on the pool table will move around, knocking into one another seemingly on their own, and the beer pump at the bar will pull forward – again, on its own.

It is not just the pub itself where activity has been noted; upstairs in the family's living area, strange sounds and sightings have been experienced by several family members. One night, one of Donna's daughters came and woke her dad, telling him that there was a 'little girl under the table' in the sitting room. Furthermore, the Donna has heard the sounds of children when her own children are either not in the building or asleep.

Donna has often felt as though she can see a figure in her peripheral vision, but as she turns, it vanishes. She also constantly feels as though she is being watched. She confessed that when she first moved into the property it used to scare her – to the point where she did not like locking up the building on her own or going to the bed and breakfast part of the building alone – but she says that now she is used to it. She has sensed that there may be a resident spirit who does not want her there and this was confirmed by a visiting medium, who told her that there is an old lady resident in the living quarters that used to live in the building and does not like to share what she considers to be *her* space. Despite this, Donna has remained determined to combat the oppressive feeling and carry on, not letting it affect her life.

As I walked through the building with Donna, she showed me each of the rooms in the bed and breakfast and we spent a few minutes in each one. She described room number one as the most haunted, as a presence of a spirit has been picked up in that room by a medium. The spirit gentleman said to occupy that room apparently

spoke through the medium introducing himself as John. The presence of John in room one had previously been sensed by psychic sensitive Steve Johnson, and he had also sensed the presence of a woman in the main living area of the house.

My EMF detector became active during my time in room number one which was interesting, as there was no obvious source of power to set it off. When I checked the audio following the time spent in that room, however, there were no sound anomalies captured at all. Interestingly, when Donna took me into room number four and I said 'Does anything ever happen

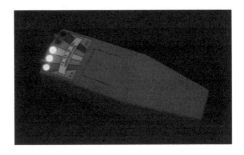

The EMF detector responding to requests to light up in Room one.

Room one, described as the most active room in the bed & breakfast.

in here?' Donna replied 'No – I don't feel anything present in this room – this room doesn't really bother me'; but upon checking the audio from our time in that room, a disgruntled male voice was picked up saying 'Get out of my room!'

Nothing unusual was captured on audio from the main living area during my visit; however, Donna said she was keen to have an investigation carried out, to try and capture evidence and also learn more about the ghostly residents who share her home. I was also intrigued, and an investigation will be taking place in the near future.

Wetherspoons – The Moon Under Water, High Street

The site of Wetherspoons has seen an extensive history with many different functions. In its early years, it was the premises of John Allen & Co. who were grocers and candle makers, then in 1885 it became the main post office for Boston, handling 150,00 telegrams and providing four separate postal deliveries each day.

The post office moved to larger premises in 1907, and the site was used as shop premises in the years to follow before becoming a bar and finally opening as a Wetherspoons bar and restaurant in 1998.

Numerous staff at this restaurant have reported the eerie disembodied sound of a woman humming and singing, emanating from upstairs. Also, glasses and other objects have been known to fly from shelves and smash on the floor with no explanation. A male apparition has been seen sitting in the snug area of the bar and, whilst no apparition has ever been seen upstairs, the staff toilet and office area have been known to generate an overwhelming feeling of a ghostly presence. This sensation has also been described by all of the tenants that have occupied the upstairs living quarters over the years.

Following my discussions with the manager of Weatherspoons about the bizarre sights and sounds and suspected ghostly presence, I will be returning at a future date to conduct an investigation.

The Moon Under Water.

6

FYDELL HOUSE, SOUTH STREET

Constructed in the early 1700s, this picturesque building (affectionately referred to as 'the grandest house in town') was purchased by Joseph Fydell in 1726. Joseph was a trader and stamped his trademark on the rear of the building, giving it the official name of Fydell House. Following his death in 1731, his nephew Richard Fydell bought the house in 1733 and built a reputation as a very successful wine merchant. He was a very influential figure in the local community where he served as Mayor, and in politics where he was elected as a member of parliament. He married Elizabeth Hall, and their son, Thomas, followed in his father's footsteps, becoming a wine trader in the family business and also becoming active in politics and parliament. The house remained in the Fydell family until 1868 and was purchased by the Boston Preservation Trust in 1934. Since then it has become a charity, open to the public, where it has been the setting for functions such as community activities, themed events, classes and weddings.

Over the years, many people have reported the general feeling of a presence within the building, generally giving reference to the area around the staircase, where there have also been 'cold spots' reported. One of the cold spots has been felt in the American Room – and one gentleman recalls an experience that took place in that room: he heard the sound of whispering in his ear when he was completely alone – as though someone was whispering to him specifically. He was not able to decipher any specific words and it happened very quickly, but it was notable enough to attract his attention, as no one else could have been responsible for the sound so, to date, the experience remains unexplained.

The first recorded testimony of a ghostly sighting, however, came from a lady who visited the building in the late 1990s and reported seeing a 'grey lady' on the stairs. The period of dress was not confirmed but it was reported to be a ghostly apparition.

A further ghostly apparition, described simply as a figure, was spotted on the balcony at the top of the family staircase in 2011. The sighting only lasted a split second; it was therefore not possible for the witness to confirm whether it was male or female, but it was long enough for them to be certain that it was a person.

The owner of Ye Old Magnet Tavern, which is situated opposite the house, has reported that the alarm seems to go off on a regular basis, outside opening hours, with no obvious trigger. She also confirmed that she has often seen a lady looking out from one of the upper floor windows at night. My enquiries led me to an explanation: the alarm being set off is apparently due to human error, according to staff at Fydell House. However, there is no explanation for the lady seen looking out of the window. The window

in question is in room one, which today is a classroom and conference room. There is a door in room one that leads to offices in the next room, where Dan Watts and his colleague once ran a small business. Dan informed me that on one occasion that door was found to be mysteriously unlocked. Only the business and Claire Sheldrake, the current manager of the house, were key holders to that room, and they were adamant that nobody had unlocked it. No explanation could be found, leaving them all baffled.

Claire Sheldrake is in no doubt that there is a ghostly presence in the house, and says she has sensed it on many occasions. She described one occasion during the summer: she was in the garden picking fruit from one of the trees, when she saw an impression of a

This picture highlights the upper window, second from right, where a ghostly female has been seen looking out late at night, when the building is locked. (Author's own photo)

'dignified man that had the appearance of a butler' walking across the lawn. It happened in an instant and the man did not communicate or acknowledge her. Claire is very objective in her views towards the concept of paranormal activity and admits that this could have been merely a trick of the light – that said, she is also mindful that the first tenant of Fydell House, Henry Rodgers, did in fact have a butler – could this have been his ghostly apparition?

Claire informed me during our interview that in her view, the bottom of the garden is the only 'uncomfortable' area of the premises in that any presences resident in the house are very friendly and this lends itself to the very discernible positive ambience around the building, which is very noticeable to visitors.

Another experience that she recalled, this time inside the building, was that one day the sound of footsteps was emanating from the Green Room (directly in front of the main entrance area). Upon going to investigate the sound, she noted that the only other people present in the house at that time were all in the kitchen and not in the Green Room – in fact, none of them had left the kitchen and therefore, the source of the footsteps remained a mystery.

The area of Fydell House specifically referred to as 'haunted' is the library, where on one occasion a visitor reading a book felt a presence with them in the room, as though someone was looking over their shoulder. Turning round expecting to see someone else in the room, the individual concerned was surprised to see that they were completely alone.

The American Room, where unexplained whispering was heard. (Author's own photo)

Elizabeth Fydell (1741-1813), granddaughter of Richard Fydell. This has been nicknamed the 'lucky' painting, as many people over the years have experienced good luck after touching it. One man even won some money on the lottery, which he attributed to having touched the painting! (Photo courtesy of Dan Watts)

Claire's love of Fydell House and her passion for preserving the history and legacy of the Fydell family was clear to see when I visited and, while she had no desire to have a spooky ghostly encounter, she was very keen to know which spirits from the Fydell family are still residing in the house and, most importantly for her, whether they approve of the way she is managing the building today. I therefore made it my mission to try and find out. I returned to Fydell House one cold winter's evening with some assistant investigators to carry out an investigation.

Fydell House Investigation – 4 January 2013

Present: Gemma King, Melissa Lawton, Dan Watts, Chloe Watts, Den Watts, Mike Shinn and Building Manager Claire Sheldrake.

The evening began with base readings of sound and EMF being taken in different areas of the building. As I walked the building with Mike, I introduced the team to any resident spirits, inviting them to come and communicate with us throughout the evening using our equipment. The only EMF readings notable at this time were in the foyer and the library.

As soon as this was complete we sat down with the group in the library and I opened the séance. It did not take long for the glass to show signs of movement, although, disappointingly it was quite laboured and slow at first. It was, however, a promising sign that there were spirits trying to communicate with us. As the upturned wine glass slowly and randomly glided and juddered around the table we felt that the spirit moving it, like most, had probably never communicated with people in this way before and was learning how to do it, resulting in these random movements. During this time we were talking amongst ourselves about all the wonderful work that Claire does, on a voluntary basis, in her endeavours to preserve the heritage of the house and Fydell family – and at this very moment, the glass shot across the board to YES. It was nice to think that the spirit was also appreciative of all Claire's hard work!

The movement of the glass was still quite laboured so we asked if our relatives that have communicated with us before in this way could come on to the board and assist any resident spirits who would like to come through. At this point, the lights on the EMF detectors lit up and the glass moved quickly to YES. A short while after this, the glass was moving but kept tipping (which is very unusual and something I have not experienced before) and Chloe had the idea to turn it the other way up in case they would find it easier to move that way. We did so and sure enough it began moving immediately. We found out that we were communicating with a little boy named 'CESAR'. He told us he was five years old and had his younger sister (aged four) with him. I felt that given his age it would be a better experience for him if we were to play a game with him rather than ask him lots of questions – I had also considered, as I normally would, that younger spirit children coming through would struggle to spell on the board. Cesar told us that there were three spirits in the room with us and confirmed that he would like to play a game (taking the glass to YES when asked) so we placed coins all around the board. I invited him to knock them all off the board and without hesitation the glass quickly glided across the table to each coin in turn, knocking them all off. At this point in the audio a very clear anomaly was captured, which sounds like the excited titter of a young child enjoying the game. (As with many EVP anomalies captured during investigations, this will be audible on the Haunted Boston website).

I needed to go to the ladies' room and said to Cesar 'Can I go for a wee – is that okay ?' The glass went to NO. We laughed and Cesar confirmed that he wanted me to stay. A bit later another team member needed to go to the toilet and as he left I joked 'Oh – you get to go for a wee – *he* gets to go for a wee !' At this point on the audio, a little child's voice is heard saying 'Do one'. We did not hear this at the time (I heard it on the audio recording when I played it back later) and I did have to go to the toilet eventually, so I asked Cesar again if it was okay and he said 'YES'. I asked him

which way the toilets were and he took the glass in that direction on the table. He seemed like a very sweet little boy.

He told us that there were four spirits resident in the building but was sadly unable to spell their names. We asked if there was a grown-up present that may be able to spell some names for us and Cesar said YES, so we thanked him for coming to speak with us and said that we hoped he would stay with us for the rest of the evening.

My own thoughts in relation to Cesar during the investigation led me to consider that perhaps he was not connected to the Fydell family but just passing and wanting to connect with us and say 'hello'. It is noteworthy that often spirits will come through to séances who are not connected to the building at all, or anyone at the table, and simply want to say 'Hello', and quite often they are children.

The next energy on the glass was not as strong as Cesar and as the glass struggled to move, I asked 'What is your name?'. At this point on the audio a male voice is heard saying what sounds like 'Bernie' but then the glass moved to GOODBYE. I said that I would love to know who the lady in the window is, and right at that moment a different energy came onto the board. It was a female, and she gave her name as Fiona. She told us that she had died a natural death at the age of ninety-four, and in spirit she permanently resided at Fydell House. She was quite a strong presence and the EMF lights were flickering significantly during our communications with her – furthermore, she moved the glass so quickly that our fingers could not keep up with it at times. She said that she had two sons – Gregory and Ben – and that it is likely to be a spirit by the name of Deane that has been seen in the garden. She gave her surname as Fydell and said that she was married to Richard Fydell. She said that Richard Fydell resides permanently in the building. Whilst Fiona was a very strong energy, I was not sure that these details would be validated by historic records as I was not aware of Richard Fydell of Fydell House being married to anyone of that name – this was something I would have to check afterwards and naturally it is disappointing in séances when you communicate with a good, strong energy but the information given cannot then be validated. We asked her again and she was adamant that she was related to the Fydell family who owned the house.

She confirmed that there are four spirits resident in the building – herself, Richard, Deane and (we assume) one of her sons.

Finally, I asked Fiona if she had a message for us and she spelled 'BE HOME SOON'. I asked her if she was being reincarnated and she said 'YES'. What usually happens is that spirits are at peace when they go into the light, and then they can exist in the spirit world and manifest their spirit in a location where they are most happy. However, they do have a choice as to whether they want to remain in spirit or live another life as a human, and many do come back. What Fiona was telling us was that she is going to be reborn in human form.

During the séance our attention was drawn to one particular corner of the room, where several investigators, at the same time, heard clomping sounds as though someone else was in the room.

After the séance we split into two groups to carry out vigils around the house. One group went to Room one where the female apparition has been seen in the window, and the other went to the American Room, where a cold spot had been reported and a disembodied whispering voice had been heard.

My group was in the American Room, and upon inviting spirits to make us aware of their presence, a tapping sound was heard emanating from the corner of the room. I invited the spirits to tap a second time for validation, but sadly no second tap was heard. After a while we moved our focus to the staircase where the female apparition had been seen. As Chloe and I sat on the stairs with our backs to the gallery window (halfway up the stairs), Claire and Mike (who were standing at the foot of the stairs) both suddenly became aware of an arm and hand waving through the window – they could not say whether it was male or

The staircase where the female apparition was seen and a cold spot is often felt. The window visible in the picture is the one from which a ghostly arm and hand were seen waving during the investigation.

The balcony at the top of the staircase, where a dark apparition figure was seen. At the top of the landing on the right is room one, where a lady has been seen from outside, looking out of the window.

female, but they were certain it was not an illusion. I was struck by the fact that Claire was adamant it was not a trick of the light as she is very objective about the paranormal activity reported, and tends to play it down if anything. I was further intrigued by the fact that the window is way above ground level and it would therefore not have been physically possible for a passer-by outside to have been responsible for the waving. I was disappointed not to have witnessed this spectacle myself, but with two very credible witnesses to the event I was left quite excited and curious about it. We sat in silence for a while on the stairs but nothing further happened so we turned our attention to the Green Room, which was also quiet – no audio anomalies were picked up at this time either.

I went out to the garden, took some photographs and captured an image of a large orb, which seemed to have the face of a lady in it. (This picture will be posted to the website).

The other group, who had been in room one, did not report any unusual events during their vigil and no EVP audio was recorded during any of the vigils.

As the investigation came to a close I concluded that there are definitely spirits present at Fydell House – but any connection to the Fydell family would only be validated by studying the Fydell family tree in more depth. When I did so, however, I was not able to validate any of the names from the séance – disappointing, as they were clearly spirits that had manifested in the house. That said, the family tree is recorded as far back as 1575 but indications are that the

The séance in the library. We had just played the 'coin game' with a five-year-old spirit boy named Cesar. Unusually, the spirits present at Fydell House seemed to find it easier to move the glass when it was positioned upright – perhaps this is due to their history in the wine trade!

Fydell family predated this, and the year Fiona gave us was 1504. This means that whilst she never resided in Fydell House itself, both her and Cesar may well have been members of the family centuries ago – but sadly we will never know.

FYDELL OF FREISTON AND BOSTON

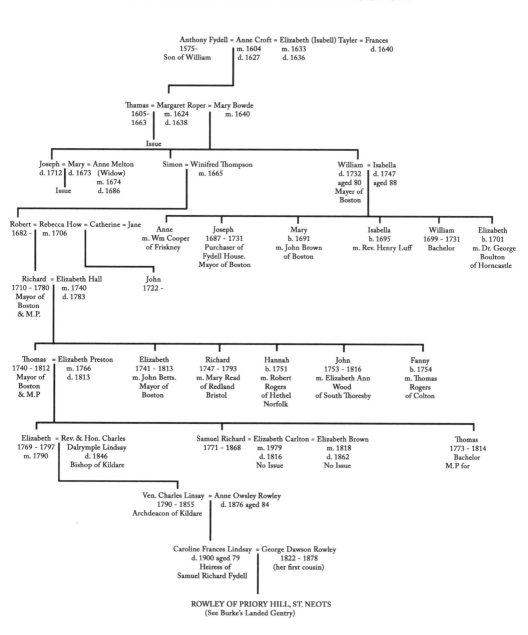

Anthony Fydell = Anne Croft = Elizabeth (Isabell) Tayler = Frances
1575- | m. 1604 m. 1633 d. 1640
Son of William | d. 1627 d. 1636

Thamas = Margaret Roper = Mary Bowde
1605- | m. 1624 m. 1640
1663 | d. 1638

Issue

Joseph = Mary = Anne Melton Simon = Winifred Thompson William = Isabella
d. 1712 d. 1673 (Widow) m. 1665 d. 1732 d. 1747
m. 1674 aged 80 aged 88
Issue d. 1686 Mayer of Boston

Robert = Rebecca How = Catherine = Jane Anne Joseph Mary Isabella William Elizabeth
1682 - m. 1706 m. Wm Cooper 1687 - 1731 b. 1691 b. 1695 1699 - 1731 b. 1701
of Friskney Purchaser of m. John Brown m. Rev. Henry Luff Bachelor m. Dr. George
Fydell House. of Boston Boulton
Mayor of Boston of Horncastle

Richard = Elizabeth Hall John
1710 - 1780 m. 1740 1722 -
Mayor of d. 1783
Boston
& M.P.

Thomas = Elizabeth Preston Elizabeth Richard Hannah John Fanny
1740 - 1812 m. 1766 1741 - 1813 1747 - 1793 b. 1751 1753 - 1816 b. 1754
Mayor of d. 1813 m. John Betts. m. Mary Read m. Robert m. Elizabeth Ann m. Thomas
Boston Mayor of of Redland Rogers Wood Rogers
& M.P Boston Bristol of Hethel of South Thoresby of Colton
Norfolk

Elizabeth = Rev. & Hon. Charles Samuel Richard = Elizabeth Carlton = Elizabeth Brown Thomas
1769 - 1797 Dalrymple Lindsay 1771 - 1868 m. 1979 m. 1818 1773 - 1814
m. 1790 d. 1846 d. 1816 d. 1862 Bachelor
Bishop of Kildare No Issue No Issue M.P for

Ven. Charles Linsay = Anne Owsley Rowley
1790 - 1855 d. 1876 aged 84
Archdeacon of Kildare

Caroline Frances Lindsay = George Dawson Rowley
d. 1900 aged 79 1822 - 1878
Heiress of (her first cousin)
Samuel Richard Fydell

ROWLEY OF PRIORY HILL, ST. NEOTS
(See Burke's Landed Gentry)

A family tree, showing descendants of the Fydell family since 1575. (Image courtesy of Claire Sheldrake and Phil King)

7

NORPRINT LTD

Now a subsidiary of Magnadata Group, Norprint are among the world leaders in labelling solutions such as supermarket products, railway tickets, electric meter payment cards, magnetic ID cards for workforces all over Europe and many other intelligent ticketing systems that use magnetic data strips.

The former Norprint (Magnadata) premises on Norfolk Street, the workplace for over 200 employees. (Author's own photo)

The company produce over 10 billion labels each year.

Whilst they have only been trading under the name Norprint since the 1980s, the history of production at their former premises on Norfolk Street dates back to the mid-twentieth century, and the story I was told about the strange occurrences at the old factory led me to visit the eerily quiet and now disused building, accompanied by Basil Wright – an employee at the Norfolk Street site for thirty years. Also accompanying me was my assistant investigator Chloe Watts.

Basil (who I came to know as Bas) told me that when he first joined the company, the building on Norfolk Street was already very old. In addition to this, he informed me that during work to remove one of the factory pillars they found footings from houses that had formerly occupied that site.

The first part of our tour took us to the downstairs office area, once busy with the buzz of administrators and telephones, but for the last five years completely abandoned and unoccupied. As we walked through the building and paused to take in our surroundings I could sense nostalgia tinged with sadness from Bas, who had experienced many years of happy employment in this now redundant and forgotten building. Bas took us to the foot of a wooden staircase in the former reception area and explained that this was the setting for one of the most significant events in the paranormal history of the site. He went on to explain that one night a security guard, on his usual rounds, was standing in reception. He was checking that all the windows were secure. He had already validated by way of his computer system that there was no one present in that part of the building – people could only gain access with swipe cards, and anyone present showed up on the central computer.

Suddenly, the room became icy cold, and as he turned around he became aware of a monk-like figure at the foot of the stairs – seemingly looking straight at him. Shocked and stunned by what he could see, he froze on the spot and could only keep his eyes on the figure to see what would happen next.

After a few seconds, the monk turned and ascended the stairs in a smooth drifting movement as though floating – he then disappeared. The security guard followed the path of the figure upstairs only to find that it had vanished – and there was nowhere it could have gone.

He was left very shaken, with cold chills, and had been petrified by the experience. When the incident occurred, he made a swift exit from that part of the building to the sanctuary of nearby colleagues (including Bas) who were working in another part of the factory. Upon seeing him they could immediately tell that something was wrong; they described him as 'white as a sheet' and 'shaken' and as he told of his frightening experience they knew from his appearance and his credibility as an individual that he was not making it up. In fact, it took him half an hour to regain complete composure.

As I stood in the former reception with my investigation gadgets and invited any resident spirits to come forward and make their presence known to me, my KII meter immediately lit up. I had literally just explained how it works to any spirits that may have been around at the time and was excited to see it light up straight away. It lit up to orange, and upon inviting the spirits present to take it up to red it progressed up through the lights all the way to red, where it remained flickering for several seconds. There was no power in the building and no source of EMF energy that could have provided an explanation for this activity. To me, this was very intriguing and quite promising in terms of finding some evidence and engaging in communication with spirits during our tour, especially given that unoccupied buildings can be especially prone to spirit manifestation.

The staircase, where the sighting of a ghostly monk left a security guard 'shaken' and 'pale'.

The factory floor, showing the path taken by the ghostly gentleman, who disappeared through the double doors to the left of the picture.

As we progressed up the stairs formerly ascended by the apparition, I invited the spirit energy illuminating the lights on my KII to accompany us and give me a tour of their building. The lights then continued to flicker all the way up the stairs. Upon entering a room on the first floor I invited the spirit to appear with me in some photographs either in full bodied form or as an orb of light – whatever they could manage – and my assistant investigator Chloe began to take photographs. Pretty quickly, large orb anomalies started to appear all around me and even on my clothing. This was fantastic to see.

The next part of our tour took us up a further set of steps to the old canteen area. Just outside the canteen is an old storage area where 'something' unexplainable was seen many years ago. Regrettably details of this sighting are sketchy as the man that witnessed the event has since passed away. However, the KII meter did light up to red in this area, again with no explanation.

As we progressed through the vast empty factory floors and long, echoing corridors with old squeaky doors, Bas reminisced about times gone by and eventually paused outside a small room adjacent to the factory floor. This room was formerly the first-aid room, and he explained that this was the location of yet another unexplainable event. A security guard was going about his daily rounds and, in the process, had found the door to the first aid room unlocked. He noted that this was unusual given that it was not possible to gain access to the room without a key, and all visitors to the room were logged on the computer system. He secured the room and moved on with his rounds – however, when he returned 5-6 hours later he noted that the door was open again. The computer validated claims that no one had been in the room and even more strangely, the bed at the end of the room had an indentation in it as though someone was lying there. Right at the moment when Bas was telling me this story, a mystery male voice was picked up on my audio device saying 'it was Jake'. Could this be a spirit friend telling us the identity of someone – a spirit gentleman called Jake – that had been lying on the bed? Or perhaps he was trying to tell us that a man called Jake that had somehow bypassed the security system and got into the room, making the imprint on the bed. Whatever the voice meant, it was wonderful to hear on the audio as it added further validation that we were not alone in the building.

Moving on from the former first-aid room, the adjacent factory had been the scene of a male apparition sighting and this is where Bas took us next. Close to the area where they had found footings of houses that formerly occupied the site, a mysterious male presence was once seen walking along the factory floor towards the double doors at the end. The man was seen to walk through the doors without opening them,

where he then disappeared. Again, this was during a time when that part of the building had otherwise been unoccupied. As the witness followed the man, he was aware that the only possible exit from that area was a roller shutter door at the end of the room that had been entered by the ghostly gentleman. However, the shutter door always made an incredible noise every time it was opened and there was no sound at all on this occasion. The witness quickly progressed through the double doors, only to find an empty room on the other side. The ghostly gentleman had completely vanished. Could this have been the apparition of an occupant of one of the houses that predated the factory on that site? – or perhaps a former employee of the factory, given the path taken and his exit specifically through the doors? Either way, this ghostly sighting in the building has never been explained.

Before leaving the building we revisited upstairs where there had previously been offices, via the staircase where the monk had been seen. We had previously had a lot of responsive KII activity in this area, and many orb anomalies captured in our photographs; this time we also heard tapping – three definite taps in the room where we were standing. At one stage, I drew attention to a key that I had seen on the floor and speculated about what it was for and, right at that moment, a male voice was captured on the audio. At this stage, Chloe and I were the only two people upstairs so there was no reason for the voice recorder to pick up a male voice. Despite the voice being at quite close range it was not easily decipherable when I played it back – although I feel it may have been commenting on the key I had just pointed out as it sounds as though the word 'key' was in the first part of the phrase.

The final part of our tour took us up a creaky, rickety staircase into a roof space right at the top of the factory. For years it was a fully functional part of the site – now only occupied by remnants of an old machine and the many pigeons who have taken up residence. When this space had been operational, staff had reported feeling very uneasy, as though someone was watching them. No one could ever work out where these feelings emanated from, although no one ever saw a ghost in that room.

The redundant Norprint building may now rattle with emptiness, however, it also echoes with the nostalgia of times gone by. So many people have come and gone over the years it is perhaps no wonder that this seemingly empty building is now buzzing with a different kind of activity.

8

SILT SIDE SERVICE LTD, LONDON ROAD

Silt Side Service Ltd. (Author's own photo)

Whilst this thriving motor factors has now moved to new premises just 100 yards from the original building, ghostly memories from the many years spent running the family business still haunt business owner Ken Bolland.

I went to meet his son Carl, who gave me a tour of the now-unoccupied former premises. He told me about the history of the location, and events over the last four decades that that had led to his father and some staff to the conclusion that their former premises were haunted.

A zestful non-believer himself, Carl explained that his father Ken had been running the business since the 1970s, spending a lot of time alone in the building and that from then until the present has seen 'more ghosts than Scooby Doo!' He went on to explain that his father would work late into the evening on most nights doing his paperwork and therefore spent a lot more time in the building than anyone else. He also confessed that whilst he had personally not seen any ghosts in the building, he had witnessed phenomena that he could not explain scientifically, such as the sounds of heavy footsteps emanating from upper floors in the building and the sound of heavy objects dropping, which he described as not dissimilar to the sound of a brick falling to the floor. He said that he would often go upstairs to explore these mysterious sounds and find that no one was up there, nothing was out of place and everything appeared as normal. Whilst these occurrences always defied explanation, Carl always remained very passive, just shrugging them off.

Whilst talking about his father's experiences, he recalled one particular occasion where a ghostly sighting prompted an investigation to locate a suspected intruder in the building, which subsequently baffled the attending police officers. It was late one evening and Ken was in his office on the third floor doing his paperwork, when he suddenly heard sounds he didn't recognise – sounds of movement and 'clomping about'. He opened the door to his office and looked out into the small corridor outside, then realised that the noise was emanating from the room to the left of where he was standing (perpendicular to his office). He opened the door to that room and was met by the sight of a male figure standing in front of him. He froze for a moment before shutting the door, running to an outside phone box and ringing the police to report an intruder. He also called Carl and another of his sons, whilst still watching the building from the phone box. The front door downstairs was, and still is, the only possible route to and from the building as there were no other doors and most of the windows were bricked up. Ken continued watching the door from the phone box until the police arrived, and when they did arrive, he was confident that no one had left the premises.

When the police arrived at the scene they bought a large Alsation dog with them to assist in checking the premises and, having learned that the intruder was still in the building, they quickly began their search starting downstairs.

The dog vigorously searched the lower floors of the building but when it came to ascending the stairs leading to the office, it would not progress further and started to whimper and cower on the floor, seemingly very scared and uncomfortable with the surroundings. One of the police officers carried the dog up the stairs to the third floor but they could not persuade the frightened animal to go any further and had no idea what could possibly have caused this reaction from a well-trained police dog.

Another strange phenomenon that occurred on a regular basis involved a soft-seated chair that was kept up on the same floor as the office where the male figure had been seen by Ken. Every morning upon going upstairs, there would be an imprint as though someone had been sitting in it. Ken would also sometimes report that when coming into the building in the morning the front door would open, then slam shut and he would feel a cold breeze rush past him on the stairs.

Ken reported seeing many ghostly figures walking about the building over the years and other members of staff also witnessed some of the other strange

This is the view that Ken had through the door where the apparition was seen. A large football-sized white orb was captured to the right of my photograph, which is perhaps more visible on the book website. (Author's own photo)

phenomena such as the sound of loud footsteps upstairs and sounds of heavy items crashing to the floor in unoccupied levels of the building. Whilst it was only Ken that witnessed the ghostly sightings over the years, other members of staff would refuse to go upstairs due to the oppressive atmosphere and unexplained noises that were emanating from upper floors. It is possible that alleged events in the history of the site may have led to the oppressive energy and presences felt mostly by Ken throughout the building, including speculation that someone hanged themselves in the old courtyard over 100 years ago following a dispute over a woman. The courtyard now forms part of the building, but was most likely to have been part of a neighbouring drinking house and stable in a previous century (when most of the street was occupied by pubs and brothels). It has also been alleged that when the building was used as a shipping port, the sailors used to come in and abuse the women of upstairs brothels and their children. Furthermore, it is said that a tragic accident took place when the building was used to store ship cargo, when someone fell down the lift shaft to their death, although the identity of this person is not known.

Whilst the exact history of the building and site is sketchy, it is known that in previous centuries the building formed part of the docks, and in the 1940s it was used for the storage of ship cargo coming in from the river. In the 1950s it was a central distribution wholesaler called Burton and Allton and was taken over by Silt Side Services in 1972.

Due to the high level of paranormal activity that took place over the years and the many stories associated with the building, team 13 Paranormal carried out an investigation. I was not present for that investigation but they have shared with me the events of that night.

Silt Side Service Ltd Investigation, 29 September 2012

The team began the investigation with a medium walk carried out by Spiritualist Medium Adrian Fuller, who visited the floors one by one. Here is a summary of his findings:

Floor 1

Adrian sensed a male character, who was looking curiously at the items on the shelves. The name Ben was associated with this character. He also sensed the presence of a family consisting of a gentleman and two children who were holding hands. A lady was present with them, but at a distance. The year 1907 was relevant to the lady and the family.

A fire was also linked to this floor and the name Wayne was connected with this.

It was sensed that food and grain was stored on this floor at one time.

As Adrian reached the end of the room he sensed a negative presence – a male who liked to scare people and laughed to himself while doing this. The name Henry Stocks was given. He was wearing an apron and had hanged himself in the building. It was sensed that it had been forty-six at the time and the year was 1924.

A lady was also picked up on this floor but she was very formal. The time period associated with her was the 1800s.

The large canister cap that was thrown across the room by an unknown entity during the investigation.

Floor 2

On this floor Adrian sensed that people would hear knocking sounds and a particular chair would move on its own. He also picked up on two men fighting – their names were Bill and Edward and the fight related to a bet which had got out of hand. This event was connected to the 1930s.

Floor 3

Here Adrian picked up on a woman tutting, and the words 'Don't go there' were said. It was sensed that the sounds of working, hammering and the tackle of boats were involved here at one time.

Floor 4

Here, Adrian picked up on a group of four or five fishermen –some with beards and wearing long socks. The names 'Sister Rose' and 'The Marclue' were thought to be connected, and the group feels they could be names of boats.

Smugglers were also picked up here, plus a woman crying who was extremely upset.

The energies of six people were felt on this floor and all were negative.

Vigils

The first vigil was held on the top floor of the building, as that is where team members said they had felt the most uncomfortable. There were two mediums present at the investigation, who did sense negative energies on that floor, surrounding everyone. During the quiet vigil a bottle top was seemingly thrown across the room. It could not have been kicked by accident as everyone in the room was standing still at the time so this event baffled the team. They conducted some table tipping in attempt to get YES and NO answers to their questions and

they did experience a lot of movement as they did this – but the mediums present at the investigation warned them that something was 'not right' and the information coming through was so upsetting to some team members that the team opted not to publish it in their report. That said, the information that came through did give the team insight as to why the spirits are still there, and why they won't leave.

While on this floor the team also made contact with a spirit, believed by the mediums to be called Joseph, who had a disability and saw out his life on that floor of the building. While the team were calling out questions to Joseph, one member ventured deeper into the large space on that floor to explore further, only to hurry back moments later,

The lift shaft where someone allegedly fell to their death. (Author's own photo)

74

The tipping table used by 13 Paranormal as a spirit communication tool. (Courtesy of Dean Grant)

reporting a sighting of a gentleman standing looking at him. The team took the table to the area where the ghostly gentleman had been seen and the table began to move quite vigorously. It was sensed by the mediums that this gentleman needed help crossing over and they were able to do this so that he could find peace.

The next vigil was held on the third floor, and the team decided to try to the table tipping again as it seemed to be the most successful method of communication in this particular building. The table did start to move quite violently in this room but the mediums commented that the team needed to

be careful as they were not only attracting the positive energies from the third floor but the negative ones from the fourth floor. Then, in a matter of moments, the atmosphere changed and the room began to get darker – this made some members of the team very uncomfortable. The EMF detectors were displaying extremely high readings and there was no explainable source for the readings, given that the building was disused at the time of the investigation and there were no sources of power nearby. As soon as the team speculated about moving to another area the EMF detector stopped flashing and the table stopped rocking.

The final investigation vigil was on the ground floor of the building. The mediums sensed the presence of a family on this floor who had once worked there. There was again significant movement of the table when the team called out to the spirits, and Team Manager Dean felt the sensation of his jacket being pulled. He opted to keep this information to himself as he did not want to influence other team members; however, shortly afterwards, team member and medium Adrian reported the same sensation and felt that it was a little girl trying to make her presence known. Staff members that were present at the investigation did report that they had seen a little girl in that area, so this was a good validation of what the team were experiencing.

The investigation ended at 3.30 a.m.

9

BOSTON TOWN – MORE GHOSTLY ENCOUNTERS

Shodfriars in 2012. (Author's own photo)

Shodfriars Hall, South Street

Shodfriars Hall was originally constructed sometime in the late fourteenth century as a monastic building. It was restored and extended into a grand theatre in 1874 by architect Sir George Gilbert Scott and his son J. Oldrid Scott at a cost of just £9,000. The restoration project saw the hall transformed into a grand entrance to the theatre, and the theatre itself could seat 650 people.

When the theatre closed in 1929, it became a billiards hall, before later being used as a restaurant and finally shops.

Now a Grade II listed building, Shodfriars Hall still contains shops, and it is from one of those stores, Mystique Boutique, that I heard a tragic story connected to the former theatre building. The story was about a young lady whom is said to have been dismissed from her job at the theatre approximately a century ago. Dismayed by her predicament, she hanged herself near the stage and is now believed to haunt the building. A former shop manager, Dawney Love, has never actually seen her but has reported frequently feeling a presence in the theatre and surrounding rooms (now empty or used for storage). She reported that quite often when she went upstairs into that quiet disused empty space she had a strong sense that she was not alone. This did not make her feel uncomfortable, and she spoke very affectionately of the building. I have to say, that following my tour of the spectacular building, where particular areas are completely frozen in time, I can see why.

Sam Newson Music Centre, South Street

Once owned by Thomas Fydell, this seventeenth Century building was a granary for over two centuries. However, in the late twentieth century, this large grain warehouse was lovingly converted into the Sam Newsom Music centre and now forms part of Boston College.

An old view of Shodfriars Theatre. (Courtesy of Billy Jenthorn)

This commemorative plaque on the wall recounts the history of the building and its beginnings as a mill when Boston's grain trade was thriving.

Many years ago, an apparition of a young female was seen looking out from one of the windows of the top floor of the building. There are also cold spots frequently reported in that area. It is believed by some that the lady may have died tragically in the building during the time when it was a mill.

The Shaw Road Ghost

In 1961 there were several sightings of a ghostly apparition on Shaw Road – in different places and at different times. The frequency of these eerie and frightening sightings led to interest from the local press at the time, the *Lincolnshire Standard*, who printed the following article:

> A ghost was seen in the Shaw Road area by numerous people and although seen at different places, times and dates the description of each was very similar. Sheila Smith, of 32 Shaw Road, said at the time, 'I was walking along Shaw road at ten o'clock at night when I saw someone walking towards me. I didn't recognise him, but was about to say good night when suddenly I realised with horror that it wasn't real. It wore dark clothes of forty years ago, and it seemed to have only rudimentary features under something like a trilby hat. It glided towards me under a street lamp, and in a second it disappeared. I know it wasn't a shadow, and it was far too close to me to be imagination. I was absolutely petrified and ran up the road towards two people I could see and then my sister came along and I clutched hold of her all the way

home.' Her mother, Mrs. Elizabeth Smith, commented : 'I've never seen anyone look as bad as Sheila did that night, but then I know what she felt like because I've seen the same figure myself. It was at about the same spot in the road, again after dark, when I sensed that someone was overtaking me. I glanced over my shoulder as this same black figure, hatted and robed but without feet, glided past me. It went through a hedge and simply disappeared. First to see the figure was probably Rosemary Booth of 18, Shaw Road, who worked in Hazell's drapery shop near her home. 'I was on the riverbank as dusk was turning into night,' she said, 'when suddenly this thing appeared. It was transparent, and I could see a tree through it. It seemed to float over the grass towards the tree, and when it got there it vanished. I can tell you I daren't go any nearer that tree and I came home very frightened indeed.' Mrs. Edna Dales of 8, Shaw Road, was faced with the apparition in her dark back garden. 'I was with our dog, when without a sound this figure, with its collar turned up and a hat on its head, and black all over, floated over the garden fence and across the grass. It went straight through the opposite hedge and vanished into the night. Brandy, our Labrador, would normally have gone for anyone in the garden after dark, but he didn't take the slightest notice.' It was on the same night that Mrs. Dale's daughter Janice saw the ghost near the Multisignals mast. 'I was with a friend when I turned round and saw a man just like my Mother told me about afterwards. I told my friend to look, but by the time she did it had gone.' Shaw Road and its environs is built on what was known for many years as Dr. Shaw's Field, and he was apparently a doctor who lived in a large house at the Fenside Road end of the field, and left this country for South Africa 120 years prior to these sightings. But while he was here he was notoriously awkward over a right-of-way that ran through the field from the Witham Bank to Boston West – could it have been Dr Shaw?

Having become intrigued by the accounts of the Shaw Road ghost, I made enquiries with the current residents to see if there had been any recent sightings of this floating eerie male apparition. Disappointingly, however, none of the current residents had seen it.

Tattershall Road

In the early 1990s, two couples had a strange ghostly experience when travelling coming home from a quiz night at the Oak Tree (now Malcolm Arms) at Antons Gowt. They progressed down Tattershall Road in their car, eventually

Tattershall Road junction as it was at the time of the ghostly sighting. The small island has since been removed. (Map data © 2012, Google)

Newspaper's impression of a ghostly apparition seen on Shaw Road. (Courtesy of the Boston Standard)

reaching a small island in the middle of the road (where there is now a right turn for Boston) and on that island they saw a figure dressed in a medieval jester's outfit, just standing there.

All four witnesses say it just stood still and looked at them, and as their car turned right it just vanished. Given that the driver of the car was sober and the passengers had had very little to drink, there was no explanation for this sighting.

Phantom Train on the A16

In 2010 a man was driving home along the A16 between Kirton and Boston at approximately midnight, and he saw what he thought was an articulated lorry with no lights at the rear. As he got closer, however, he could see it was the back of a guard's railway van.

He initially thought it was on a low loader, but then noted there was no other vehicle so he pulled out to have a better look. It then became apparent that it was an old-fashioned steam train pulling several carriages. As he came toward the street lights, it disappeared. The A16 was built in the 1990s; however, it was originally a railway line, closed in the 1960s.

'3 Bridges' Midville Road/ Fodderdyke Bank

Along this stretch of road between New Leake and Stickney, there are three bridges crossing Hobhole Drain and Fodder Dike in close proximity to one another. A ghostly apparition of a man with his dog has been seen by numerous people in this area, walking off a bridge and into the road.

The area known as '3 Bridges'.

Lovelaces Florist, Market Place

Lovelaces on Market Place has been in existence as a florist for approximately fifteen years, and has been run by Vicky and Maxine throughout that time.

There are several ongoing unusual occurrences in the current shop - most notably that flowers are knocked off shelves by an unknown source, when they are positioned very carefully and the weight of a display or flower bucket is such that it would take a strong force to knock it down. Furthermore, baskets are suddenly knocked down from the ceiling, with no obvious cause, and objects inexplicably fall from shelves in the back store room.

Another unusual phenomenon is that the bell sometimes rings on the door - as though someone has entered the shop – but when Vicky or Maxine go to check, there is no customer. The radio also mysteriously changes channels quite often.

The most notable occurrence in the shop was when a woman was seen walking through the shop at a time when there were no customers – she was a ghostly apparition and was described as a small elderly lady. Could she be the spirit of a former resident of the building or former customer of a shop that once existed there? Maxine and Vicky will always remain curious, but told me that they never feel threatened by the activity and don't mind sharing their space – particularly if it is with a nice elderly lady.

Lovelaces.

Boston Guildhall Museum

One of several spectacular medieval buildings remaining in existence today, the Boston Guildhall has a history dating back to the 1390s. The structure has seen little change over the last 600 years.

In that time it has had many different functions, such as a court, jail, council chamber, town hall, restaurant, and museum. It was even owned by Henry VIII in the early sixteenth century. Furthermore it is believed to be the place where William Brewster, William Bradford and their followers (the Pilgrim Fathers) were taken in 1607 following their arrest while trying to flee the country for Holland, on a

Boston Guildhall Museum.

quest for separation from the Anglican Church and religious freedom abroad. Perhaps most gruesomely, it was one of the locations where the bodies of deceased plague victims were stored centuries ago.

Today, as you walk around the Guildhall, remnants of the building's illustrious history adorn every room. With original relics and many features once in regular use and now beautifully preserved, such as the medieval court room and two of the former prison cells below, you can literally feel six centuries of history in the atmosphere.

Over the years there have been many unusual experiences reported within

the building from staff and members of the public, to inexplicable banging sounds, full bodied apparitions and anomalies appearing in photographs. Intrigued by this, I went to the Guildhall myself to explore its past in more detail and speak with the staff there to hear the eerie accounts of ghostly events first hand.

I was told a story by a member of staff who, one morning, had seen a very unusual-looking old lady. This staff member had only just opened the building for visitors, and was aware that a couple of people had entered the building and were looking around together as she went to make her morning cup of tea. On her way to the kitchen area, she passed the old prison cells on her left and, as she did so, she saw a couple on her right and an elderly lady on her left, seemingly in her own world; her eyes transfixed on the prison cell that she was staring into. She seemed unaware of anyone else around her.

The member of staff smiled endearingly as she recalled:

> What immediately struck me about this lady was that she was so beautiful. Despite being in her late seventies – perhaps even eighties – her skin was so radiant, and I thought: 'What a beautiful old lady'. Of course, what also struck me about her was the way she was dressed; she was wearing a grey suit and heeled boots with laces that were clearly not from this time period. I thought it was very strange.

When she returned with her cup of tea, the old lady had gone. Upon going back to the reception desk, the staff member asked her colleague, 'Have you seen the old lady?' Her colleague at the reception desk looked confused and questioned, 'What old lady?' The member of staff replied 'The old lady that was looking around'. Still confused, the receptionist replied 'There isn't an old lady – the only people that have come in to look around so far are that couple'.

Totally stunned by this, the member of staff wanted to know who that old lady was and if anyone else had seen her. As the couple were leaving the museum she asked them 'Excuse me, have you seen an elderly lady? I was showing her round and I think she may have got lost'. The couple told her that they had not seen anyone else in the building at all, and the old lady was not seen again that day. That said, she has been seen on several other occasions in that area of the building, sometimes walking into a prison cell and disappearing. Despite several reported sightings of her, however, her identity still remains a mystery, and it would seem that the prison cells themselves have their own share of ghostly presences, with mysterious inexplicable voices often heard emanating from them.

Impression of a female apparition by prison cells (Courtesy of Andrew Malkin). An apparition of a man holding a lantern was captured in an investigation photograph. However, in order for the picture to be fully appreciated in detail, I opted to publish this on the book website instead of the book itself.

Another very chilling paranormal event was encountered by a former curator of the museum one quiet Sunday when he went upstairs to the old council chamber to sit and finish some paperwork. As he sat at the large table, engrossed in his work, he suddenly became aware that he felt very strange – as though he was being watched. He developed hair-raising tingles on the back of his neck and began to feel extremely uncomfortable. Upon looking up, he discovered he was not alone at the table – it was surrounded by other gentlemen, who were all sitting in silence staring at him. He was so rattled by this experience that he hurriedly fled the building and resigned from his role as curator a short time later.

In addition to that apparition sighting, there have been quite a few testimonies over the years relating to the council chamber, mostly of visitors and staff feeling very uncomfortable in there. A strange indescribable sighting in a dark shadowy corner reported by one visitor left her so frightened that she apparently ran out of the museum. In another incident, some contractors working in that room late at night suddenly became overcome with feelings of dread, coupled with a notable drop in temperature. Like the frightened female visitor and the petrified curator, they also packed up their belongings and hurriedly left.

Upstairs, close to the council chamber, some American visitors once bore witness to another paranormal event while touring the building. As they passed through a narrow walkway towards the Banqueting Room, a flurry of papers inexplicably flew from one side of the walkway to the other. There was not a breeze at the time and in fact, no doors or windows were open – the event was a complete mystery. The American tourists were quite impressed by it; they thought it was a stunt set up for their entertainment.

In between the council chamber and the office is the Buttery – another area reported to emanate an oppressive and uncomfortable atmosphere. An apparition of a woman has been seen hanging from the rafters in this room but it remains a mystery who she was and how she came to die in this horrific way.

On my visit to the Guildhall, I myself experienced something unusual. The time was 3.12 p.m., a little before closing time, and I was upstairs in the Banqueting Room taking photographs. I was standing very still, trying to get a good angle on my lens when I suddenly felt a violent thudding sensation around my feet – as though someone was stamping on the floor right next to me or beneath the floor banging upwards. It was so powerful that the floor physically shook beneath my feet. As I felt the *thud thud thud*, I looked around casually expecting to see someone else in the room – perhaps heavy-footed older children – but there was no one anywhere. There were two other gentlemen in the museum, but they were in a different part of the building at that time. I did not hear the sound that accompanied the thudding sensation because there was a loud audio tape playing throughout the museum at the time, as there usually is during the day, re-enacting events that would have taken place in olden times. This drowned out all other noise. In view of this I cannot really say any more about my experience and what it could have been. There is, of course, the possibility that it could have been vibrations from a heavy vehicle passing on the road outside. However, the feeling was much more like individual 'thuds' than a vibration, and

I therefore kept an open mind. Upon going back downstairs in the museum I reported feeling that sensation in the Banqueting Room to staff and it transpired that others have also experienced this strange phenomenon in that area – this was echoed further by former visitors of the hall that I spoke to after the event. A degree of banging and creaking can be expected in any building as old as the Guildhall; however, another story of a banging sensation beneath the floor that was not explainable came from a former member of staff who had been 'spooked' while sweeping down a small spiral staircase with a dustpan and brush. As she made her way down each wooden step, she suddenly heard and felt loud banging underneath her on the inside of the steps, which gave her such a fright that she ran out of the room. The wooden staircase is hollow and it was believed that there was once a cupboard under there. The bangs that people hear and feel are the bangs of an angry man locked in there, desperate to get out.

The building had been investigated previously by 13 Paranormal and that investigation night produced some excellent photographs containing not only orb anomalies, but in one case, a full bodied apparition.

Medium Adrian Fuller had felt a strong negative energy upstairs in the Buttery. He had sensed an angry spirit who would make noises and make his presence felt to scare people away. He felt that bodies may have once been dragged along the floor in this room, with possible connections to a grave robber who took the jewellery from deceased victims – people brought in from the street that had perished in the plague. During the vigil in this room, another team member began to feel uncharacteristically sad and she sensed the presence of a sad lady dressed in grey. The team called out to her and after a while began to hear noises that they could not explain or recreate – such as the sound of someone climbing the metal ladder propped against the chimney breast.

The Guildhall has seen diverse functionality and much activity over the centuries of its existence and will no doubt continue to baffle attendants in future years as memories from the past continue to remain very much alive within its stone medieval walls.

The staircase, where knocking was heard and felt from underneath. (Author's own photo)

Geoff Moulder Leisure Complex, Rowley Road

This highly popular fitness centre and swimming venue is a hive of fun sporting activity during the day. By night, however, it becomes subject of a completely different form of activity – of the ghostly kind.

Staff working at the swimming centre have witnessed many unexplainable events, some of which have left them quite unsettled and fearful of venturing into particular areas on their own. In an interview with David Horry, Principal Leisure Services Officer, he explained that most of the activity seems to focus around the training swimming pool (not the main pool). He said that the staff do not like to enter that area on their own when the lights are off, as they feel a strong sense that they are not alone. A figure has been seen by many staff, usually between 9 p.m. and midnight, sitting by the vending machine. David recalled that during the twenty-year period he has spent working in the building he has seen the figure many times when locking up. They are so confident that there is a male ghost there that they have even given him the name George.

Other mysterious occurrences include showers and taps inexplicably being turned on, seemingly by themselves, and objects being thrown about, knocked down from shelves and broken. On several occasions there have been numerous items broken, and this has resulted in the staff believing that there is an intruder and calling the police. Cleaners of the building recalled that on one such occasion they heard strange noises, as if objects were falling from shelves and smashing on the floor; this was accompanied by a cold draught. Upon checking the building, they found

The main swimming pool.

that the internal doors all remained as they had been left – closed and locked. The police were called and when they arrived on-site with their dogs to conduct a search the building was found to be empty, with no explanation for the draught, noises or broken items.

Upon hearing reports of the strange occurrences at the leisure centre, Dean and his team from 13 Paranormal wanted to try and uncover the full story behind the entities making their presence felt around the building and so they attended the site to carry out an investigation.

Please note that some details of the investigation, such as spirit names, remain unpublished so as to respect the privacy of any family members that may still be living.

Adrian on his medium walk. He sensed an injustice surrounding a little girl's death in the pool many years ago. (Courtesy of 13 Paranormal)

Geoff Moulder Leisure Complex Investigation – 16 January 2010

The team members present at the investigation were: Dean Grant, Adrian Fuller (medium), Scott Grant, and Shona Crampton.

At the start of the investigation, Adrian took time to pace the building, to see if he could pick up on any spirits present. Straight away in the swimming pool area he was able to sense the spirit of a girl who had drowned in the pool. In addition to this, he connected with an angry spirit: that of a policeman. The policeman was unable to find peace, and was telling Adrian that this was because he had been involved in the case of the drowning of the little girl and he felt it had not been resolved.

When Adrian moved on to the office area, he picked up on a mischievous spirit who would move and throw things about. Interestingly, the team had not previously been aware of this phenomenon taking place and it was not until after the investigation that this was validated by staff at the leisure centre.

Following Adrian's psychic walk, the team set about their vigils and began by setting up a trigger object in the office area. It was a glass, which they placed on paper and drew round to see if it would be moved.

During the vigil that took place alongside the larger of the two swimming pools, the team heard strange sounds as though someone was jumping into the pool and swimming. They also heard a noise, as though someone was walking around the pool.

The second vigil took place alongside the smaller of the two pools (the training pool where staff of the complex have sensed an uncomfortable presence) and during this vigil, Adrian connected with the policeman again and was told that 'the truth has yet to be revealed about the case'.

While conducting this vigil, the team asked various questions and invited the spirits to knock in response. This had some surprising results, with several knocking responses being heard.

The final vigil took place in the old female changing rooms and was attended by David, the Complex Manager. During this vigil Adrian connected with a spirit called Derek, who had apparently followed them from the swimming pool area. Knocking sounds were heard in response to questions during this vigil, but in addition to this, EVPs were also captured; when talking to one of the spirits one team member said 'I know you suffered and everything', and a female voice was captured at this time on the audio responding 'Yeah'. Also, when a team member said 'I know how you feel', a response was captured that said 'No, you don't'. These responses had not been heard by anyone at the time of the investigation and were only picked up during audio playback.

When the team moved on to the shower area, investigator Shona felt a sensation of someone touching her hand. In order to seek validation of this experience, she asked for her hand to be touched again and, not only was the sensation felt again, but at that point in the video footage a mist formation in the shape of a hand is visible hovering over Shona's hand.

The trigger object that had been placed in the office had not moved during the investigation night; however, unexplained knocks were heard in that room during the vigil.

In summary, the team considered the investigation at Geoff Moulder Leisure Complex to be very insightful in that the activity experienced and captured on their recording devices, together with the additional insight of medium Adrian, seemed to validate the testimonies of activity experienced over many years by staff working in the building.

P&M Framing, South Street

This picture framing shop has been in the Colbert family for eighteen years, and during that time many inexplicable events have occurred that have manifested a strong belief and acceptance that they are not alone and have uninvited guests of the ghostly kind.

The strange occurrences are not confined to the shop; they also emanate from the Arbor Club, a drinking club located on the upper floor of the building, directly above the shop. The most common phenomenon noticed is that during the day, at times when the club is unoccupied, locked and alarmed, strange sounds can be heard. The current owner of P&M Framing, Mandy Colbert, explained:

P&M Framing, South Street.

One particular day, I was in the shop talking with a friend and suddenly heard footsteps above us and chairs scraping – as though someone was moving all the furniture about; and I thought: Ah – John's back – I need a word with him. My friend offered to keep an eye on the shop for me, but as I ran out the shop, undid the door and ran up the stairs, all the alarms went off.

Both Mandy and her friend had been in no doubt that there was someone upstairs, but had there been anyone present upstairs the alarms would have gone off before, and would not have been activated at all had the owner of the Arbor Club been present.

As well as the sounds that emanate from the upper part of the building, Mandy and the staff at the picture frame shop experience a lot of instances of objects being moved about. Mandy also recalled a particular occasion where her car key went missing and following an intensive but fruitless search of the shop, her son brought a spare key so they could drive the car home. However, the next morning upon arrival at work she found it very quickly under the small waste bin by the shop counter. She was shocked and baffled at the discovery, given that the bin had been lifted and replaced no end of times during the meticulous search the previous day.

Objects are regularly disappearing and reappearing in a different place at P&M Framing and Mandy recalled that she arrived at the shop one morning to find that a cleaning spray had been placed in the middle of her work bench. She knew that it had not been left there the night before because she routinely cleans everything down and tidies everything away at the end of each working day. She knew that the previous day had been no different.

In addition to the objects that are moved about, it would seem that their ghostly friend also likes to make their presence known by interfering with the radio. Apparently, the radio (when in use) switches itself off at 11 a.m. every day…and then back on. There is no alarm set, or any other function that would cause it to do this, and the staff have been completely shocked by it – in fact one member of staff was so freaked out that they no longer put the radio on when she is working!

There have also been many occasions over the years where they have heard the shop door open and sensed someone walking into the shop, only to go through from the workshop to serve and discover that no one is there at all.

When Mandy described all of the unusual events that have taken place during the years that she has spent running the shop and her father before her, she added: 'Whoever the presence is, he's not a horrible person. Nothing bad has ever happened – and we don't feel anything bad when he is here'. We actually joke with him now, when something goes missing, saying "OK, where have you put it?!"'

Mandy was recently told by a spiritualist medium visiting her home that she has a mischievous ghost in her workplace who likes to play jokes. Naturally she was not surprised by this, and does not mind the frequent ghostly intrusion as she continues to run her family shop.

Poundstretcher, Market Place (former Scala Theatre)

In 1913-14, Scala Theatre was renovated from a book shop and printers, which dated back to 1855. The architect, Mr Frederick Parker, FSA transformed the building into the first ever purpose-built theatre and cinema in Boston and it boasted a grand auditorium, a balcony, a restaurant and winter gardens in the foyer, where an orchestra would play. Sadly it closed in June 1940 for cleaning and repairs, and never re-opened to the public. The building was used for the training of RAF airmen and troop concerts during the Second World War and the café did remain open until 1950; however, the building was then taken over by numerous shops, including a furniture store. It is currently a Poundstretcher store.

The stairs leading to the original theatre balcony are still in existence today, and the various testimonies of unexplained noises and strange activity that has been reportedly emanating from the upper floor of the building since the 1980s would indicate that there may be spirit presences from this former hub of social activity still enjoying their heyday in the grand theatre.

The first known testimonies came from staff working at Cavendish Woodhouse – the furniture store that occupied the premises in the 1980s. They said they could often hear footsteps coming from upstairs in the auditorium, but they always tried to convince themselves that the noises were actually coming from adjacent buildings. However, since that time, a further testimony came from a builder who said that he had been doing some work upstairs in the auditorium when his tools started to mysteriously disappear and reappear in a different place. As a non-believer in 'ghosts', he found himself questioning his scepticism and reluctantly confessed to have been somewhat freaked out by the incidents of moving tools and the general atmosphere up in the auditorium that he encountered while going about his work.

Staff who work in Poundstretcher today have also admitted that the upper

Scala Cinema. (Picture courtesy of Helen Shinn, the Boston Old Times)

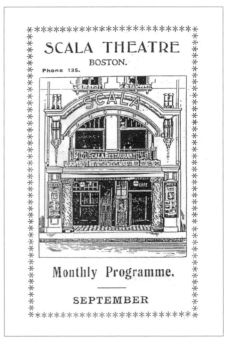

Theatre Programme. (Picture courtesy of Helen Shinn, the Boston Old Times)

The orchestra in the foyer of the Scala Theatre, which was known as the Winter Gardens. (Picture courtesy of Helen Shinn - the Boston Old Times)

floor of the building seems to have a 'spiritual presence'. A paranormal investigation was held in the theatre by a group called Paranormal-Lincs (paranormal-lincs.co.uk), who found evidence of intelligent spirits – in the form of EVP, such as a responsive answer 'Behind you, at the back' to a question posed to spirits about their location in the theatre – and photographic anomalies showing large orbs. They also captured residual EVP, where the words 'plates and cutlery', 'cream', 'Corporal and Army' and 'Airmen' were recorded – all reflecting a century of history contained in the fabric of the building. Their conclusion was that whilst there is clearly residual energy in the building and some intelligent spirit manifestation, there is nothing negative about the atmosphere at all and the spirits present do not mean any harm.

AFTERWORD

For as long as I can remember I have been passionate about listening to people's ghostly testimonies, researching different theories relating to ghostly manifestations and, in recent years, investigating paranormal phenomena first-hand in haunted locations.

I am on a quest to find out why they are haunted, provide insight and reassurance to residents of those locations, assist any spirit friends in need of help and capture evidence of both paranormal activity and the afterlife. I have now investigated many haunted locations, locally and further afield and there are still so many that I have yet to explore; like other investigators all over the world, I hope that I will one day be able to capture physical evidence, irrefutable to the most hardened of sceptics, of the existence of ghosts.

I have met many wonderful people throughout the course of writing my books, and when out giving talks on the subject of paranormal investigating and the various types of ghost manifestation. I have been asked many questions over the last few years. The most common questions I have been asked are 'Have you ever had a ghostly experience?' and 'Don't you get scared?' Well, I have to be honest and in both cases say, 'Absolutely, yes!' The best experience I have had to date has been hearing the ghostly but beautiful sound of a young child humming right in front of me, which brought tears to my eyes because it was so lovely to hear. That said, I have also had unpredictable and potentially dangerous events occur such as a stone being thrown close to me. Some say that spirits can't harm you; however, unpredictable events such as glasses flying from shelves in pubs and people being physically touched, or in some cases pushed, have led me to disagree with that theory. Whilst nothing of that nature has happened to me so far, you have to expect the unexpected when out on investigations. It can sometimes be a little unnerving, sitting in dark cellars inviting spirits to come and interact with me, or walking around creaky dark unfamiliar places during the night using my various gadgets to attract the attention of ghosts. However, my passion for capturing evidence of ghosts far outweighs the fear factor, and I have to say that if I came face-to-face with a ghost now, I would be scrambling in search of my investigation gadgets rather than the nearest exit! As I continue on my enigmatic journey and quest for answers and evidence, I hope people will enjoy reading the ghostly experiences and stories that are contained within the pages of this book and sharing further pictures, ghostly audio clips and videos that I have uploaded on to my book website. I would like to leave you with this chilling thought: statistically more non-believers and sceptics will have a ghostly experience in their lifetime than those who believe; but whether you are a believer or not, how would you react if any of the spooky events from this book happened to you?

Gemma King, 2013

BIBLIOGRAPHY AND FURTHER READING

Felix, Richard, *The Ghost Tour of Great Britain* (Lincolnshire: Breedon Books Publishing Co. Ltd, 2009)

Harden, Gillian, *Medieval Boston and its Archaeological Implications* (South Lincs Archaelogical Unit, 1978)

King, Gemma, *Haunted Spalding* (The History Press, 2012)

Ormrod, W.M., *Boston Blackfriars: From Priory to Arts Centre* (Pilgrim College, 1990)

Peatling, David, *Goin' to the Dance: A Personal History of the Boston Gliderdrome* (David Peatling, 2003)

Wright, Neil, *Boston: A Pictorial History* (Phillimore, 1994)

Wright, Neil, *The Book of Boston* (Barracuda Books Ltd, 1986, second edition 1991)

WEBSITES

https://sites.google.com/site/hauntedbostonbook/ (website to accompany book)

www.13paranormal.co.uk: 13 Paranormal are a non-profit scientific paranormal investigation team who investigate locations all over the UK and also invite guests to join them on some events

http://www.bostonpast.blogspot.co.uk/

www.bostonuk.com: information on local history.

http://www.fydellhousecentre.org.uk

http://www.ghosts.monstrous.com/

www.midlandparanormal.co.uk: Midland Paranormal Investigations (MPI) are a non-profit paranormal investigation team who investigate locations all over the UK. They are scientific and professional in their approach to investigating claims of activity, placing emphasis on capturing visible and audible evidence of paranormal phenomena.

www.paranormal-lincs.co.uk: Lincolnshire-based paranormal investigation team.

If you enjoyed this book, you may also be interested in…

Haunted Spalding
GEMMA KING

Spalding's ghostly side is explored in detail in this book, which recounts the paranormal occurrences around the town and their impact.

A very active pub spirit, a family who resorted to exorcism to rid themselves of a malicious presence and cheeky spirits at a sports club all feature.

Gemma King has long been passionate about the paranormal, and here she undertakes her own investigations in an attempt to unravel the mysteries of Spalding.

9780752469928

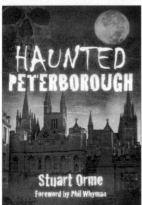

Haunted Peterborough
STUART ORME

Peterborough is plagued by ghostly occurrences. Ghostly children, phantom monks and a restless cavalier all stalk the town, and the author explores their origins – and their legacy.

This book also contains detailed accounts of the spectres and stories of Peterborough Museum, one of Britain's most haunted buildings.

Stuart Orme is the creator of the Peterborough Ghost Walk and an expert on the town's history – some of what he has uncovered will surprise you…

9780752476544

Haunted Scunthorpe
JASON DAY

Haunted Scunthorpe guides you through the town's paranormal hotspots and follows the apparitions into the surrounding villages and beyond. Including previously unpublished haunting accounts from the author's own case files, this collection of local hauntings and has something for everyone, from the layman to the hardened paranormal investigator. It is guaranteed to entertain and spook anyone interested in Scunthorpe's ghostly history. Writer and broadcaster Jason Day was born and raised in Scunthorpe, where he lived for nearly thirty years.

9780752455211

Visit our website and discover thousands of other History Press books.

www.thehistorypress.co.uk